THE GUNSMITH

474

Outlaw's Gun

THE GUNSMITH

474

Outlaw's Gun

J. R. Roberts

SPEAKING VOLUMES, LLC
NAPLES, FLORIDA
2021

Outlaw's Gun

ISBN 978-1-64540-574-0

Chapter One

Clayton Black had a reputation to uphold.

As far as outlaws went, his reputation put him at the top of the list. That meant he was wanted by both sides of the law. The lawmen wanted to put him away, while other outlaws wanted to pad their own reputations by killing him.

In the town of Raton, New Mexico, he could feel eyes on him in the Wayfarer Saloon, as he stood at the bar over a beer. Since he'd been through this many times before, he knew he was not going to be able to just walk out of the saloon. What he didn't know was if he would be dealing with the law, or not.

He waved the bartender over.

"Getcha somethin'?"

"Is there any law in here?"

"No," the bartender said. "In fact, our sheriff's outta town, right now."

"Okay," Black said, "thanks."

"If there's trouble," the barman said, "I've got a shotgun behind the bar."

"That's okay," Black said. "If there's trouble, I'll handle it."

"Suit yerself."

He went to the other end of the bar to serve other customers.

Black kept his eyes on the mirror behind the bar and, sure enough, three men stood up from their table and approached.

"Clayton Black," one of them said.

Black turned and looked at the men.

"Come on, Clay," the speaker said, "you remember me."

The man was in his thirties, his face covered with back stubble that Black had to see through.

"Dick Shepherd," Black said.

"That's right," Shepherd said. "I rode on one job with you, and then you cut me loose."

"Because you were useless," Black said. "That was . . . what? Ten years ago?"

"I was young," Shepherd said. "You could've taught me."

"I didn't have time to waste with you," Black told him.

"Well," Shepherd said, "you're gonna pay for that now."

"Don't be a fool—" Black started, but it was way too late.

Shepherd went for his gun, and his two partners followed his lead. Black drew quickly and fired several shots. Shepherd went down, and his two partners followed.

Black holstered his gun, turned and picked up his beer.

"Mister," the bartender said, pointing, "you been hit."

Black looked down and saw that he was bleeding from his left side.

"Ah shit . . ."

***

"You were lucky," the town doctor said. "The bullet seems to have gone right through without hitting anything vital. The problem is the exit hole. It's clean, but bigger. Once I finish sewing you up, you're gonna need to take some time to heal."

"I've been shot before," Black said. "I can heal in the saddle."

"That might've been true in the past, when you were younger," the sawbones said. "You ain't gonna heal as fast, this time."

"Whataya sayin'?"

The doctor, who was in his sixties, at least ten years older than Clayton Black said, "I'm sayin' don't get shot no more. The next one could be fatal."

"They can all be fatal, Doc," Black said.

"Especially at your age," the doctor said.

He finished patching Black up and allowed him to put a fresh shirt on.

"Now take my advice," the man said, "and stay off a horse for a while."

"I can't stay in this town, Doc," Black said. "People know I'm here, and if they hear that I'm injured, they'll come running."

"So what are you going to do?"

"I'll have to ride out and find someplace else to lay low," Black admitted.

"Well," the doctor said, "once you do, if I was you, I'd make some changes in my life."

"Oh, I plan to." He took the Navy Colt from his holster. "Part of the reason I got shot is this gun. It's old and heavy, and it slowed me down. So I'm gonna get me a new one." He holstered it, again.

"Mr. Black," the doctor said, "that's not exactly what I meant about making changes in your life."

"I know what you meant, Doc," Black said, "but changes have to come a little at a time." He paid the man. "Thanks for your help."

Chapter Two

Two months later . . .

When Clint Adams rode into Tylerville, Montana, he had no idea he would be meeting one of the most infamous outlaws in the country. But that would come later . . .

***

Ever since his money had been stolen out of the bank several months before, he had been taking jobs now and again which would help him to pad his poke. Just such a job had brought him to Tylerville.

He didn't hire out his gun, just his services, this time as a bodyguard and escort. He was to bring a girl named Ellie Winston to meet her husband-to-be, Angus Tyler, who owned—among other things—the town of Tylerville. Clint had picked her up from a boat in San Francisco, prepared to transport her to Tylerville by buggy. But Ellie—who was from England—said she was an expert horsewoman and insisted on riding the entire way. So, using some of the expense money Tyler had sent him, Clint bought her a horse.

He tried to buy her a mild-mannered mare, but she chose a spirited Piebald, with black spots on white.

The eleven-hundred-mile trip had taken them the better part of three weeks. Ellie had refused to shorten the trip by using the railroad. She wanted to see the country she was going to be living in.

That wasn't all she wanted. The woman—who Tyler assured Clint was a sheltered lady—turned out to be an adventurous . . . wench, was the only word Clint could think of. Especially after she crawled into his bedroll with him on their second night out.

**

They had camped in a clearing under a full moon. On their first night they had sat up late at the fire and talked, with him answering all her questions about the "Wild West" she had heard and read so much about. She was fascinated to discover that he was friends with such men as Wild Bill Hickok, Bat Masterson and Wyatt Earp. Dime novels about those men had made their way across the pond to England. And that included dime novels about the Gunsmith.

On the second night, however, the auburn-haired beauty had been curiously silent, until she simply bid him "good-night" and rolled herself up in her blanket and bedroll. However, no sooner had Clint done the same. When the girl was right there next to him, with her blanket still wrapped around her. But it soon became evident she was naked beneath it.

"Ellie—"

"Shhh," she said, sliding her hands down the front of his pants, "I have a feeling I know what kind of life I'm going to be leading once I marry a rich, older man. I want to enjoy this journey as much as I can."

She grasped his already hardening penis and Clint remembered his instructions from Angus Tyler. "Give her anything she wants!"

Together, they yanked his trousers down to his ankles, and, without even removing his boots, she slid on top of him and took him inside her hot, wet pussy.

She rode him as if she was trying to win the Kentucky Derby!

From then on, they shared a bedroll every night, until on their final night when she said, "I hope you don't think, after all this time, that I'm in love with you, Clint."

"The thought had never entered my mind," he told her.

"And you're not in love with me, correct?"

"Not at all."

"Because that would make what I have to do very difficult."

"What you have to do?" he asked.

"Yes," she said, "marry Angus Tyler. I mean, after all, he has paid all my expenses to this point, don't you agree?"

"I do," he said.

"Excellent."

She had snuggled up to him at that point and fallen asleep.

***

He delivered her to her husband-to-be the next morning, and she had thanked him very formally for escorting her there. Angus Tyler, a short, grey-haired man in his sixties, paid Clint the remainder of his fee, which was a healthy sum. Clint had taken his money and got himself a room at the Prescott Hotel. After three weeks, he was looking forward to a night or two in a real bed, not to mention a good meal.

He tackled the meal first, getting himself a steak dinner at a decent restaurant down the street from his hotel. Tylerville was a growing town, so he was going to have the opportunity to try several restaurants and cafes before he decided to leave.

After the steak, he walked across the street to the brightly lit Astoria Saloon, which had girls, gambling and beer aplenty. He decided to partake in the beer, but not the other two on his first night in town. He was still feeling pleasantly worn out from keeping Ellie happy on the trail.

He was on his second beer when one of the saloon girls moved up alongside him.

"Are you Clint Adams?" she asked.

"Yes, I am," he said, looking at her. She was a small, young, pretty blonde.

"There's a man in the back who would like to buy you a drink," she said.

"Is that right?"

"He asked me to invite you."

"Where is he in the back?" Clint asked, craning his neck to look over the crowd.

"I'll take you." To the bartender she said, "Al, two beers."

The man drew them and handed them to her. They looked huge in her hands.

"This way," she said.

As she made her way through the crowd, they seemed to part to let her pass, and she never spilled a drop of the two frosty mugs.

He finally spotted the table he thought she was heading for, and he was surprised. He had never met the man before, but he recognized him.

"Adams," the man said, "I'm glad you accepted my invitation."

The girl put the beers down on the table, and the man put a few coins in her hand.

"Thanks, darlin'." He looked at Clint. "Have a seat."

Clint sat.

"What's the Gunsmith doin' in Tylerville?" the man asked.

"I could ask the same question of Clayton Black."

"Please," Black said, "no names. Nobody here knows me, and I'd like to keep it that way."

"Whatever you say," Clint said. "What's on the mind of one of the most notorious outlaws in the West?"

Chapter Three

"Notorious?" Black asked. "Is that what I am?"

"That's what your reputation says."

"And yours says you're a cold-blooded killer."

"Touche," Clint said. "I delivered something today. It was just a job."

"So you're free now?"

Clint smiled.

"These days I'm never free."

Black shifted in his chair and grimaced.

"What's wrong?" Clint asked.

"I took a bullet a while back," the outlaw said. "It still smarts."

"It'll ache for a while," Clint said. "As a reminder to be more careful."

"I'll be more careful," Black said, "but I can't get any younger."

"Ah," Clint said, "you're feeling your age."

"Don't worry," Black said. "You'll get there."

"I hope you're right," Clint said. "Who put a bullet in you? Some lawman?"

"Some upstart," Black said. "He and two of his friends pushed me. I killed 'em, but I took one." Black scowled. "Ten years ago, when I was your age, it never would've happened."

"So why are you buying me a drink, Mr. Black?" Clint asked.

"I saw you at the bar and recognized you," Black said. "And then I had a thought."

"Which was?"

"You're not only called the Gunsmith," Black said, "you are one, right?"

"I am," Clint said, "though I haven't used those skills in some time."

"Maybe you'd like to?"

"Meaning what?"

Black took his gun out and laid it on the table.

"This gun has served me well over the years, but that's just it. It's been years. I need a new one. I'd like you to make it for me."

Buy a new gun?" Clint asked, eyeing the Navy Colt on the table. "Something lighter, but just as deadly."

"I don't just need a new gun," Black said. "I need to *be* faster."

"You need to be younger," Clint said. "I can't help you with that."

Black laughed.

"We all need to be younger, but you're right," Black said. "Age is my problem. I need you to help me fight it."

"What can I do?"

"You're the fastest gun alive," Black said.

"That's debatable."

"Okay," Black said, "you're the fastest gun in town. You can make me a new gun and help me use it faster."

"How would I do that?"

"Work with me," Black said. "I'll do anything you tell me to do."

"Here? In this town? Aren't you afraid somebody will recognize you? Or come for you? What's the price on your head, these days?"

"Who knows?" Black asked. "A thousand? Five thousand?"

"Dead or alive?"

"Of course," Black said, "but not in Montana. I'm not wanted here."

"How long have you been here?"

"Weeks," Black said. "I needed a place to lie low and heal."

"And the local law?"

"I've avoided him," Black said. "His name's Marshal Boon Davis."

"I don't know him."

13

"So you've never been here, either."

"I've been to Montana before," Clint said, "but not here."

"We could find someplace outside of town," Black said, "so that our target practice won't attract any attention."

"Your reputation is for robbing trains and stages and banks," Clint said. "I've never heard anything about you and your gun."

"I was okay," Black said. "I could use a gun, and often did, but only to stay alive. I ain't never killed anybody during a job. That's the God's honest truth."

"Then why's the price so high on your head?" Clint asked. "That's usually reserved for killers."

"The railroads can afford it," Black said. "Several lines have pooled their money."

Clint took some time to study the man.

"I'll pay you," Black said. "I'll pay you well."

Clint had known many outlaws in the past. He even liked some of them. A man lived his life the way he felt he had to. He had never held that against anybody, except for cold-blooded killers.

"Whataya say, Adams?"

"Why not?"

Chapter Four

"So you'll do it?" Clayton Black asked.

"I'll think about it," Clint said, "and let you know tomorrow."

"Well," Black said, "I'm gonna look for a place for us to work, just in case you say yes."

"I don't have a problem with that," Clint said. "Is there a gunshop in town?"

"Yeah," Black said, "I've passed it a time or two, but I haven't gone in, yet."

"Okay," Clint said, finishing his beer, "thanks for the drink and I'll see you tomorrow."

"For breakfast?" Black asked.

"Let's make it lunch," Clint said. "I'm at the Prescott. We can meet there at, say, two."

"Okay," Black said. "I'm staying in a rooming house at the far end of town."

"Are you sure nobody's recognized you, yet?"

"Positive," Black said.

"Well," Clint said, "we recognized each other, so it can happen."

"If we're together," Black said, "I don't think anybody would try anything."

"Let's hope nobody's that brave," Clint said. "See you tomorrow afternoon, Black."

"Call me Clay."

Clint nodded and gave the man a little salute before leaving the saloon.

***

Back at his hotel Clint got himself comfortable, removing his boots and unbuttoning his shirt.

There was no bed post, so he set his gun on the table next to the bed, within easy reach. He sat with his back against the wall, his arms folded. Meeting Clayton Black had been interesting, as was the man's request. The last time Clint had worked on a gun for someone, and worked with them to increase their skill, was Roxy Doyle, who had gone on to be known as Lady Gunsmith. Clint was still not sure he had done Roxy any favors.

But Clayton Black already had a reputation, and apparently, he was worried about defending it and wanted Clint to help him. But the man walked on the wrong side of the law. What would that make Clint if he helped him? Would he be considered on the wrong side of the law as well?

He didn't think so. After all, he wasn't helping Clay Black pull any robberies. He would only be helping the man stay alive.

If he didn't help him, and Black was shot down, Clint would feel responsible. Men with reputations—no matter what side of the law they were on—had to be able to defend themselves.

In the morning he'd check out the gunshop.

***

Clay Black watched the little blonde saloon girl peel off her dress, and then walk to the bed naked. He stared at her little, pink-tipped titties and the patch of golden hair between her legs.

"God, you're a pretty little thing," he said to her. "What's your name again?"

"Mary."

"And why would you wanna spend time with an old man like me?" he asked.

She ran her hand over his bare chest and said, "You're not that old."

"I'm fifty-five," he said. "What are you? Twenty?"

"I'm twenty-two," she said, then reached and grasped his hard cock, "and you don't look a day over fifty."

Chapter Five

In the morning Clint woke, feeling refreshed from a night on a real mattress. Now all he needed was a good breakfast. He washed, got dressed, strapped on his gun and went downstairs. The hotel had a small dining room with about six tables. None of them were occupied, so he took the one furthest from the door.

"Ham-and-eggs," he told the waiter.

"Comin' up, sir."

The man brought him a pot of coffee, a basket of biscuits and some butter while he was waiting.

By the time Clint started eating, two other tables were occupied, also by hotel guests. One man looked like a drummer, who put his sample case on the chair across from him. The other guests appeared to be a middle-aged husband-and-wife.

Clint ate his breakfast slowly, enjoying every bite. His last few breakfasts on the trail had been beans. Once he was done, he paid his bill and went to the front desk.

"Yes, Sir?" the natty clerk asked.

"I understand there's a gunshop in town. Can you tell me where it is?"

"Yes, Sir," the man said. "Just go out the front door, turn left and walk three streets. You won't miss it. The front window is filled with guns."

"And is the owner of the shop also a gunsmith?"

"Yes, Sir," the clerk said. "He can do anythin' you want done to a gun."

"Okay, thanks."

Clint left the hotel and followed the desk clerk's directions. He came to the window which was, just as the man had said, filled with guns. But from what Clint could see, not very many of them were in good working condition. As he entered the shop, it looked more like a junk store than a gunshop.

"Can I help ya?" a man asked, from behind a glass counter.

"I *was* looking for a gun," Clint said, "but it looks like you mostly have junk."

"Hey, I've got some good guns here," the man said. He was middle-aged and as dirty as the guns in the window.

"Really?" Clint said. "They're sure as hell not in the window."

"Guns get stolen out of my window all the time," the man said. "That's why I keep junk there."

Clint glanced around.

"It doesn't look that much better in here," he said.

"Well," the man said, "it's the only place in town to buy a gun, so what are ya lookin' for."

"Never mind," Clint said. He started to leave, then stopped. "Wait, maybe there is something you can do for me."

"What's that?"

"I might like to use your tools."

"What tools?"

"Gunsmithing tools."

"You don't need no tools," the man said. "I can do whatever you want."

"I doubt it," Clint said. "I just want to know if I can come here and use your tools, if I need to."

"Why should I let ya do that?" the man asked. "Who're you, anyway?"

"My name's Clint Adams."

The man stared at him, and his manner immediately changed.

"Geez, Mr. Adams," he said, "of course you can use my tools if ya want. I'd be honored."

"That's fine," Clint said "Thanks."

"So, when d'ya wanna come in?" the man asked.

"I'll let you know," Clint said. "What's your name?"

"Oh, it's Pete Wilcox."

"I'll let you know, Pete," Clint said. "I'll let you know real soon."

He turned and left.

Wilcox waited ten minutes, then hurriedly closed his store and headed for the marshal's office.

***

Town Marshal Boon Davis looked up from his desk when his door slammed open.

"Goddamnit, Pete, what's the all-fire hurry?"

"Do you know who's in town?" the gunshop owner asked.

"Lots of people."

"I mean Clint Adams!"

"The Gunsmith?" Davis frowned. "Now, when did he get here?"

"I dunno, but he was just in my store."

"What would the Gunsmith want with your junk shop?" Davis asked.

"He says he may wanna use my tools."

"What tools?"

"My gunsmithing tools," Wilcox said. "They don't only call him the Gunsmith. He *is* one."

"When does he want to use the tools?"

"He says he'll let me know."

"Well," Marshal Davis said, standing up, putting on his hat and gunbelt, "maybe I'll just have to find out before that."

Chapter Six

Marshal Davis figured to find Clint Adams in one of the saloons. Even at this early hour, the saloons were open for early drinkers. One of those early drinkers was the marshal.

He didn't find Adams in the Astoria Saloon but had a beer while he was there. Then, instead of checking the other saloons, he decided to talk to the bartender.

"Al, did you know that the Gunsmith was in town?" he asked.

"Sure did," the bartender said. "He was in here last night."

"What was he doin' here?"

"Drinkin'," Al said, "until Mary came over and took him to a table."

"Why?"

"There was some feller there who wanted to buy him a drink."

"What feller?"

"Beats me," Al said. "Ask Mary, when she comes down."

"When will that be?" the marshal asked.

"Try back this afternoon," the bartender said. "Maybe Adams will even be here."

"Okay," Marshal Davis said, "I'll try back, then."

The bartender wondered if he should have told the lawman that the second man was upstairs with Mary at that moment?

***

Clint didn't want to spend any part of the afternoon in a saloon. He would do enough drinking at night. Instead, he decided to wait for Clay Black at the hotel.

He was sitting in a chair in front of the hotel when Clay Black came along.

"Have you given my offer some more thought?" the outlaw asked.

"Is that what it was? An offer?" Clint asked.

"Well, it wasn't a demand," Black said. "It was . . . a favor."

Clint stood up.

"Let's go have lunch and talk about it."

"I know a place," Black said.

"Lead the way," Clint said.

Black took Clint to a small café that was hidden away on a side street.

"How'd you find this place?"

"A young lady brought me here."

Clint assumed the young lady was the blonde from the saloon. The place reminded him of the dining room in the hotel, with only a few tables.

Black recommended the steak sandwich, and they each ordered one.

"So?" the outlaw said. "What are you thinkin'?"

"I don't see any real reason why I can't do you a favor," Clint said. "If I say no and then I hear you got killed, I'll always feel it was my fault."

"You and I both know that when we get killed it'll be our own stupid fault," Clay Black said. "I'm just tryin' to put that day off a little longer."

"I can't blame you for that," Clint said.

"So," Black asked, "what's first?"

"We have to get rid of that Navy Colt on your hip," Clint said. "You're still carrying a single-action gun. Switching to double will automatically increase your speed."

"I've had this gun a long time," Black said, looking down at his hip.

"You can keep it for sentimental reasons," Clint said, "you just can't wear it anymore. That is, once we get you a new one."

"At the gunshop in town?"

"I'm afraid not," Clint said. "I took a look at it, and it's a junk shop."

"Then where do we find a gun?"

"I still have to figure that out," Clint said. "Meanwhile, we also have to get you a new holster. I notice yours is pretty worn."

Black shrugged.

"Came with the gun," he said.

"That explains it."

The waiter brought them their sandwiches, packed with onions, and a beer each.

"Good call," Clint said, after his first bite.

Black nodded his agreement.

"There's one other thing," Clint said.

"What's that?"

"I'm going to check in with the local law," Clint said. "It's something I do. But I won't mention your name."

"That's okay with me," Black said. "I suspect you've always got a target on your back."

"A big one."

Black nodded.

"I'll do that when we finish up here," Clint said. "Then we can meet up later at the saloon."

"I appreciate this, Adams," the outlaw said.

Chapter Seven

Marshal Davis looked up from his desk as his office door opened and Mary, the saloon girl, came in. She was wearing a simple cotton dress with a shawl around her shoulders.

" 'afternoon, Marshal," she said. "Al said you were wantin' to talk to me. I have to go to the general store, so I thought I'd stop in and see you."

"I appreciate that, Mary," Davis said. "Take a seat."

The pretty little blonde sat down.

"I understand you talked to Clint Adams in the saloon last night," Davis said.

"That's right," she said, "but only to give him a message."

"What message was that?"

"That somebody at a table wanted to buy him a drink."

"And who was that?"

Mary looked uncomfortable.

"I don't know if I should say," she replied.

"Now Mary," he said, "I'm the law, here. If I ask you a question, you have to answer it. That's the way it works."

"Well . . . it was a man named Black."

"Black?" the sheriff repeated. "That's a pretty common name, Mary. What's the first name?"

She hesitated, then said, "Clay."

"Clayton Black?" Davis recognized the name. What he didn't need was to have the Gunsmith, and an outlaw, in town at the same time.

"What did they talk about?" he asked. "Do you know?"

"No," she said. "I only delivered the message and served them both beers. I didn't hear what they talked about."

Davis studied the young woman, decided he had gotten everything she knew.

"Okay, Mary," he said. "That'll do. Thanks for comin' in."

She stood up but hesitated before leaving.

"Did I get anybody in trouble?" she asked.

"No, Mary," Davis said, "you didn't get anybody in trouble."

That seemed to relieve her, and she left. Davis sat back and figured the only person who might be in trouble was him.

***

The next time the marshal's door opened, he was still thinking about his conversation with Mary. He didn't recognize the man who entered.

"Can I help ya?" he asked.

"Marshal," the man said, "I'm Clint Adams."

Davis tried to hide his apprehension.

"Mr. Adams," he said, "I heard you were in town. In fact, I went lookin' for you this mornin'."

"Well," Clint said, "I thought I should check in with you. I just got here yesterday."

"I appreciate that," Davis said. "Why don't you have a seat and tell me what you're doin' in town."

"Actually," Clint said, "it won't take that long." But he sat. "I'm just passing through."

"Funny," Davis said, "that's not what I heard."

"Oh? What did you hear? And from who?"

"I heard you have a friend in town."

Clint frowned.

"Not that I know of."

"Clayton Black? The outlaw?"

"Black?" Clint said. "That's odd. I just met him last night. I certainly wouldn't call us friends."

"Is that right?" Marshal Davis asked. "Why would a stranger want to buy you a drink?"

"I think he just wanted somebody to talk to," Clint said.

"Talk about what?"

"I think that's between him and me, Marshal." Clint stood up. "I just came in to let you know I'm in town."

"What I'd like is for you to let me know when you're leavin' town," Davis said. "The both of you."

"I suspect," Clint said, "it won't be long."

As Clint Adams left, the marshal took a bandana from his desk drawer and mopped his brow. He hoped Adams hadn't been aware of how nervous he was.

***

Clint stopped just outside the marshal's door. He certainly was aware of the man's nerves, but he had to hand it to Davis, he handled it well. Now that the lawman knew about Clay Black's presence in town, Clint agreed with him. It would be a good idea for both he and Black to leave town before the word got around. There was always somebody just stupid enough to want to try to make a name for themselves.

As he walked away from the office, he also thought they were going to have to go somewhere else to find a new gun for Clayton Black. There was no way they were going to find anything in Tylerville. Once he told the outlaw the marshal knew he was there, it wouldn't be hard to convince him they should leave.

Chapter Eight

Later in the afternoon, Clayton Black entered the Astoria Saloon and was immediately approached by Mary.

"I'm so sorry," she said.

"Bring me a beer at my table," he said, "and then you can tell me what you're sorry about."

He went and sat and waited for Mary to bring his beer.

"Sit," he said, as she stood over him. "What are you sorry about?"

"The marshal questioned me today," she said. "I had to tell him your name."

"Why was he interested in me?"

"He wasn't," she said. "He was askin' me about Clint Adams."

"Ah," Black said, "I get it."

"I'm so sorry," she said, "but he's the law—"

"Don't worry about it," he said. "He probably would've found out I was here anyway."

"Is this a problem?" she asked.

"I think Adams and I will be leavin' town," he said. She pouted.

"You better go back to work, kid," he said.

"Will I see you tonight?" she asked. "Or are you leavin' today?"

"I don't think we'll be leavin' until tomorrow."

That seemed to make her happy.

Black was half finished with his beer when he saw Clint Adams come through the batwing doors.

As Clint sat across from Black, Mary hurried over with two more beers.

"Thanks, kid," Black said.

"I just came from the marshal's office," Clint said.

"I heard," Black said. "Mary told him about us."

"It's just as well," Clint said. "We're not going to find what we need here."

"I told her we'd probably be leavin' tomorrow," Black said.

"Will your horse be ready?" Clint asked.

"He's fine," Black said.

"I'll pick up a few things from the general store," Clint said.

"Sounds good. Um, you're not planning on leaving Montana Territory, are you?"

"As long as you're not wanted here," Clint said, "we might as well stay."

"That's what I was thinkin'."

"We could head for Butte, or even Bozeman," Clint said. "We're bound to find what we need in one of those places."

"I'd prefer Butte," Black said. "Bozeman's a big town, more chance we'll be recognized."

"Okay," Clint said, "then we'll try Butte first."

"Leave at first light?" Black said.

"I'll meet you in front of the general store," Clint said. "Might see you back in here later tonight."

Clint stood up and reached into his pocket for some money.

"I got it," Black said. "Next round's on you."

"Deal."

Clint left the saloon, hoping Clay Black would be able to keep out of trouble. He didn't want word getting out that they were both in Tylerville.

***

"You see 'em?" one of the three men seated together on the other side of the room asked.

"I see 'em," the second man said, "but I'm not interested in either one of 'em."

"Are you kiddin'?" the first man asked. "This is the chance of a lifetime."

The first man was in his twenties, while the other two were ten or twelve years more seasoned than him.

"You're crazy," the third man said. "That's Clayton Black right there. You understand that? Clayton Black! He's a killer."

"And the other one's Clint Adams," the second man said. "The goddamned Gunsmith! You're crazy if you think about goin' up against either one of them."

"Well," the younger man said, "not alone."

"Then you better look for somebody else to help you," the second man said.

"You two are just scared."

"You bet we are," the second man said.

"Scared and alive," the third man said.

"Well," the first man said, "I'm gonna find somebody who ain't."

"How?" the second man asked. "We rode into town together, and we don't know nobody else here. How are you gonna find somebody to go against them with you?"

"There's gotta be somebody in this town who ain't scared!" the first man said.

"You mean somebody as stupid as you?" the second man asked, and both older men started to laugh.

"I ain't stupid!" the first man said, jumping to his feet. "You'll see!"

He turned and stormed out of the saloon.

Chapter Nine

Mary stopped at Black's table.

"I don't need another beer."

"No," she said, sitting across from him, "I'm here to warn you."

"About what?"

"Did you see that young man who just ran out of here?" she asked.

"Stormed out, is more like it," Black said. "I suspect he had a fight with his two friends."

"Yes," she said, "a fight about you and Clint Adams. He wants to . . . well, kill you."

"You mean he wants to try," Black said. "What about the other two?"

"They admit that they're scared," she said.

"That's good. The one who ran out, he's younger than the other two, isn't he?"

"Yes," she said, "he looks a few years older than me."

"Well," Black said, "let's hope he lives to get a little older." He reached out and patted her hand. "Thanks for the warnin'. You should go back to work."

She smiled and moved away.

Black drained his beer, stood and left the saloon.

***

When the knock came Clint still had his gunbelt on. He kept his hand by it as he walked to the door.

"Who is it?"

"Clay Black."

Clint opened the door slowly. Then more swiftly when he saw the outlaw standing there.

"What's on your mind?" he asked.

"I think we should discuss it inside."

Clint nodded and backed away to allow the man to enter.

"What is it?"

"I wanted to let you know there were three men in the saloon watching and talking about us."

"And?"

"One of them is very young," Black said, "and probably very stupid."

"And the other two?"

"Scared."

"That's good."

"But the young one, he may be a problem."

"You really think so?"

"Oh, I don't mean he's a real danger to either of us," Black said, "but he may do somethin' to force one of us to kill him before we leave."

"The marshal wouldn't like that."

"No, he wouldn't."

"Do we know this young man's name?" Clint asked.

"No."

"Well," Clint said, "we could both stay in our rooms until morning."

"That would be hidin'," Black said. "That goes against the grain."

"I know, but—"

"I have somebody else's room I can stay in," Black said, "and I wouldn't be hidin'."

Clint smiled.

"Do you think the young lady will mind?"

"Not at all," Black said.

"Thanks for letting me know," Clint said. "With a little luck, we'll see each other in the morning."

"When the general store opens," Black said.

"Yes," Clint said, "unless we want to leave with no supplies."

"That wouldn't be smart," Black said, "since we'll be campin' on the trail."

"Right."

When Black left the room, Clint closed and locked the door. Just as he suspected—and expected—there was an idiot with a gun out there. Staying inside might have been hiding, but right now, it was the smart thing to do, if it only kept him from killing the fool.

Clint usually had a book or two with him to help while away the time in hotel rooms. However, at that moment he didn't have one. So he would pass the time breaking down his weapons, cleaning them, and putting them back together.

***

Clay Black walked back to the saloon, keeping a sharp eye out on the street. You never knew when a fool with a gun would take it into his head to shoot you in the back.

When he got to the front of the saloon, he turned and examined the street. He could see the general store, where he would be meeting Clint Adams in the morning. It made sense to spend the night in Mary's room, rather than all the way at the other end of town in a rooming house.

Might as well make that little blonde happy before they left Tylerville.

Chapter Ten

In the end, Clint couldn't just hide in his room, no matter how smart a move it would have been. So he walked to the Astoria Saloon, got a beer from the crowded bar and found his way to Clayton Black's table.

"Couldn't stay away, huh?" Black asked.

"I don't always do the smart thing," Clint admitted.

"Well, I doubt some foolish kid is gonna challenge us both at the same time," Black commented.

"I hope you're right," Clint said. "What about his two friends? Are they here?"

"Still holdin' down their table," Black said. "They've had a lot to drink."

"Let's hope they don't change their minds and find some courage at the bottom of their glasses."

Clint and Black did some serious drinking of their own and discussed guns and reputations.

"As I told you," Black said, "the railroads have made me out to be much worse than I am. I mean, come on, Jesse James robbed trains, and he was made out to be a legend and hero—at least, in Missouri."

"Are you saying you're a legend and a hero?" Clint asked, rolling his eyes.

"Oh, no," Black said. "I ain't lyin' to you, Clint. I'm an outlaw, for sure. I just ain't the monster the railroads make me out to be. What about you? The newspapers are always sayin' what a deadly killer you are."

"You can't believe everything you read," Clint said.

"Exactly!" Black exclaimed. "That's my point."

The man suddenly grimaced and sat back.

"The wound?"

Black put his hand over his side.

"They told me the bullet probably didn't hit anythin' vital, but I'm thinkin' it nicked a rib. Sometimes it's painful just to breathe."

"I've been shot a time or two myself," Clint said, "so I think I know how you feel."

"I'm probably too damn old now to be holdin' up trains," the man said. "I just want to keep myself alive a bit longer."

Clint studied Clay Black's face. There were lines across his forehead he had earned over the years, some grey hair at his temples. Except for looking too thin— probably a result of his bullet wound—the man seemed to be in decent shape for his mid-fifties or so.

"You seem to be wearing the years pretty well," Clint said.

"Oh, I ain't sayin' I'm an old man," Black said. "Just too old to do the things I used to do."

"Aren't we all," Clint said.

Clint was starting to feel the effect of his drinks and was thinking about turning in when a group of men came through the batwing doors, causing a bit of a stir.

"Know them?" Clint asked.

"Just one of 'em," Black said. "That's the kid I was tellin' you about."

"Looks like he managed to round up some help."

"Yeah," Black said, scowling.

***

The kid's name was Emmett Cochran, and he had, indeed, rounded up some help. He led four other men to the table where his two friends were still seated.

"Well?" he said. "I found some men who ain't afraid."

"Not of an old gunfighter, and an even older outlaw," one of the men said. The others laughed. They all looked to be in their twenties.

Cochran's two friends, Ollie and Jason, had drank enough that they were almost impressed with the younger man's stubbornness.

"You ain't gonna challenge them right here and now, are ya, Emmett?" Ollie asked.

"Why not?" Emmett asked. "They been drinkin', ain't they?"

"Oh yeah," Jason said, "they been drinkin', all right."

"Then seems to me they're just ripe to be taken," Cochran said.

"Both at the same time," Ollie commented.

Cochran puffed out his chest.

"That'll just make it a better story."

"And when are ya gonna do this?" Jason asked.

"After I buy my friends, here, a beer," Cochran said.

"Well, then," Ollie said, "pull up some chairs."

***

Clint and Clay Black watched the men take seats at the table and order beers.

"Maybe they're not interested in what we think they're interested in," Clint said.

"Oh, they are," Black said. "Remember what you said about courage at the bottom of a glass? That's what they're after. And they might just convince the other two to join them."

Chapter Eleven

"We could get up and walk out," Clint suggested.

"That would just look like we're runnin'," Black said. "And that wouldn't look good, would it?"

"No."

"Then we should probably just sit here," Black said, "and wait."

Clint was starting to think he should have stayed in his room after all.

***

Mary listened to the conversations when she served the drinks, and then went to Clay Black's table.

"What are they sayin', Mary?" Black asked.

"They're tryin' to convince the other two to join 'em," she said. She looked at Clint, then back at Black. "They're gonna come after you—both of you. They think you're . . . old."

"They're probably right," Black said.

"Older than them, anyway," Clint said.

"Mary," Black said, "be ready to keep yourself out of harm's way."

"I will."

She walked away.

"Now I wish I had somethin' other than this Navy Colt," Black said.

"It'll have to do," Clint said.

"Well," Black said, "it always has."

"I'd like to be able to talk them out of their stupidity," Clint said.

"Good luck with that."

***

"So, whataya say?" Cochran asked, Ollie and Jason. "Will you help us?"

"Who are these fellas?" Ollie asked, indicating the other four.

"I found them in one of the other saloons," Cochran said, "and we sorta became friends."

"And you're all ready to back Emmett's play?" Jason asked.

"Sure, why not?" one of them said.

"We'll all go down in history," another said. "That's better than livin' here the way we are."

"And how's that?" Ollie asked.

"Bein' nobody," another man said. "We're tired of bein' nobodys."

Ollie looked at Jason, both rather bleary-eyed from whiskey and beer.

"Nobody wants to be a nobody," he said.

Cochran smiled.

"We should get this done before the marshal shows up."

He stood and, followed by the other six men, walked to the table where Clint Adams and Clayton Black were sitting.

***

"What took you so long?" Black asked.

The table was against a wall, so the seven men formed a semi-circle.

"The two of you should stand up," Cochran said.

"How old are you?" Clint asked.

"What's that got to do with anythin'?" Cochran demanded.

"You have the wisdom of youth," Clint said, "which is no wisdom at all."

"You sayin' I'm dumb?"

"That's what we're both sayin'," Black said. "You're stupid, and you're bein' followed by men who are even more stupid."

"Or drunk," Clint said.

"That's enough talk," Cochran said.

"Really?" Clint asked. "Look around you, kid. Look who you have backing your play."

He had to give the kid credit, he never did look around. The other men, though, turned their heads and looked at each other.

"You think I'm stupid," Cochran said, "but I wasn't stupid enough to come over here alone. And I'm not stupid enough to take my eyes off of you."

"Son," Clayton Black said, "if me and Clint Adams stand up, you won't live another day to keep bein' stupid."

"Go ahead," Cochran said, "stand up, then. We'll show these people what'll happen."

Chairs scraped the floor, and tables were overturned as customers sought cover, because they knew there was about to be a whole lot of lead flying.

Clint and Black exchanged a glance. They knew that Clint would be working right, and Black would be working left, according to where they were positioned. They didn't have to speak.

Clint just hoped Clayton Black's Navy Colt still had life in it.

Chapter Twelve

The seven men backed up as Clint and Clay Black got to their feet. Clint could see that all of them had enough whiskey and beer in them to do this. There was no talking them out of it.

Very quickly he recalled Black saying how they both knew they would die stupidly. They should have remained in their rooms until morning. But now, because there was so much stupidity in them, men were going to die.

Clint kept his eye on Cochran. It was that young man's move that would dictate what happened.

Luckily for Clint, and especially Clay Black, there wasn't a fast gun in the bunch, just drunken egos. Clint even had time to see, from the corner of his eye, that Black was fumbling that cumbersome Navy Colt from his holster.

Clint drew his gun and made the quick decision to do something he rarely did. He fanned the gun, his left palm working the hammer, firing six shots in quick succession. The seven men were all jerked back by the hot lead, none of them getting the chance to clear leather with their guns.

It was deathly quiet after the sound of shots faded away. Clint quickly ejected all six shots from his gun and reloaded in case someone else had any ideas.

More slowly, Clay Black did the same. Clint knew if Black had been alone, he'd be dead. He had managed to kill one man, hit possibly two, while Clint was sure he had killed six. If he had been alone, he would probably be dead, since the seventh man surely would have shot him. Stupid, just amazingly stupid . . .

The onlookers moved forward to stare down at the dead men, then in open awe at Clint and Clay Black. When the batwing doors opened, Marshal Boon Davis came rushing in, gun in hand. He stopped when he saw the tableau laid out in front of him.

"It was fair, Marshal," the bartender said. "Them seven called the play."

Mary came out from behind the bar where she'd been hiding with the other girls and rushed to Clayton Black's side.

Marshal Davis walked over to Clint and Black, having to step over the bodies to do so.

"I'd like to talk to the two of you in my office, if that's all right with you gents," he said.

"None of this is all right with me, Marshal," Clint said.

"We'll be there, Marshal," Black said.

"I have to get this cleaned up," Davis said. "Let's make it half an hour."

"Agreed," Black said.

Clint stared down at the seven bodies.

"I'll be in my hotel until then," he said.

"Come upstairs," Mary said, tugging on Black's arm.

"You heard the lady," Black said. "I'll be upstairs."

Black followed Mary to the stairs, while Clint walked out the door.

***

Clint got to the marshal's office first. He decided to have a look at the man's desk while he was there alone. He found a whiskey bottle in a drawer, along with an extra gun. In another, a stack of wanted posters. Right on top was one for Clayton Black. He was wanted in three states and/or territories for robbery, but not Montana Territory.

He closed the drawer and got out from behind the desk as the door opened and the marshal walked in.

"Adams," he said. "Where's Black?"

"I assume he's on the way here."

Davis sat behind his desk.

"Are you friends with him?" he asked.

"I wouldn't say that."

"But you drink with him."

"Yes."

"Why?"

"I told you once before," Clint said. "My relationship with him, whatever it is, is our business."

"Now it's my business," Davis said. "Look Mr. Adams, I admit dealin' with you makes me nervous. Dealin' with the both of you is worse. But I have to do my job."

"I don't have a problem with that," Clint said.

"Will Clayton Black have a problem?"

"I guess we'll see when he gets here."

Marshal Davis opened his drawer and took out the top wanted poster.

"You know he's wanted, don't you? For a big price."

"Not in Montana Territory."

"No, that's true," the lawman said, "but why would you be involved with a wanted man?"

"I suppose because we're in Montana Territory," Clint said, "where he and I are equal."

Davis frowned.

"That's not an attitude I expected the Gunsmith to have," he admitted.

The door opened and Clayton Black entered before Clint could offer an explanation for his attitude.

Chapter Thirteen

"It was totally their idea," Clayton Black said. "Ask the saloon girl, Mary. She heard them talkin'."

"So neither of you had any contact with them before this?" the lawman asked.

"No," Black said.

"None," Clint said.

"So you killed seven men you'd never seen before?"

"Seven men who came at us with guns, Marshal," Black said. "That's what we saw."

The marshal looked at Clint, who only nodded. The lawman sat back in his chair and sighed.

"Okay, you can go."

Clint and Black left the office.

"We better turn in," Clint said.

"I could use another drink."

"You need my help," Clint said. "Without me you would've been dead tonight."

"Why do you think I need another drink?" Black asked.

"Your move with that Navy Colt was terrible," Clint went on.

"And your move, fannin' that Colt the way you did? That was somethin'."

"Something you should never do," Clint said. "Look I want you to turn in. I don't want either one of us shooting anyone else, tonight."

"All right."

"I'll meet you in front of the general store, as we planned."

"Okay," Black said. "Why are you bein' so pissy?"

"Because I killed six men tonight," Clint said. "Like the marshal said, men I didn't even know. That doesn't sit right with me."

"I'm sure you've had to do it before," Black said.

"It never sits right with me!" Clint said.

"Okay!" Black said. "I get it. I'll see you in the morning."

As Black walked away Clint knew he was going back to the Astoria. He only hoped the man would be able to get to Mary's room without any more trouble.

He walked the other way, to his hotel.

***

"That was amazing, what you did tonight," Mary said, as she undressed.

"I didn't do squat," Black said, tossing his boots across the room. "That was all Adams."

"He couldn't have killed all seven himself," Mary said.

"Maybe not," Black said, "but he got six of 'em, for sure."

"You only got one?"

He took the Navy Colt out of his holster, almost tossed it across the room, too.

"This cannon is good for nothin', anymore."

"Are you gonna get a new gun?" she asked, slipping into bed.

"A new gun," Black said, "and a new gun hand, if the Gunsmith has anythin' to say about it."

He set the gun and holster aside, got undressed and into bed with the young saloon girl. She put her hands on him right away.

"Are you really leavin' tomorrow?" she asked.

"We are."

She stroked his cock and asked, "Is there any chance you can take me with you?"

"No chance at all, girlie," he said, sliding his arm around her and pulling her close, "so lets you and me make this a night to remember, huh?"

He pushed her head down to his hard penis.

***

Marshal Boon Davis went to the undertaker's office. The man had the seven dead men stacked up in the back like cord wood.

"Is that any way to show respect?" he asked.

"They're dead," the undertaker said. "They don't know how they're bein' treated. Besides, I don't have the room. And I gotta have the boxes made."

"Yeah, okay."

"Who's payin' for the other burials?" the undertaker asked.

"The town."

"So no headstones, then?"

"No headstones," Davis said, "just wooden crosses. Unless some families show up."

"What about them that did it?"

"They're leavin' town in the mornin'," Davis said.

"Now, if I had the Gunsmith's body in here," the undertaker said, rubbing his hands together, "I'd treat it with some respect."

"Sorry," Davis said, "the Gunsmith is gonna be somewhere else when he gets it."

"Too bad."

The marshal just hoped, for Clint Adams' sake, he didn't get it sooner for consorting with Clayton Black, than later.

Chapter Fourteen

When Clint got to the general store the next morning it was not yet open, and Clayton Black wasn't there. He dismounted to wait, folded his arms and stared into the distance.

"Waitin' on me?" a voice asked.

He looked up and saw the front door of the general store had opened. A man was standing there, smiling.

"I've got a few purchases to make before I leave town," Clint said.

"Well then, come on," the man said. "You'll be my first customer of the day."

Clint followed the man into the store. He was placing his purchases on the countertop when Clayton Black walked in.

"Take a look here," Clint told him, "and see if I'm missing anything."

Black examined the items.

"Looks like you got the basics," the outlaw said. "Coffee, beans, jerky, some ammo . . . nothing that would make us need a pack animal."

"That's the point," Clint said. "I just want us to be able to carry these things ourselves." He turned to the man behind the counter. "Would you put these items into two gunny sacks?"

"I can do that."

"Add a couple of cans of peaches, will ya?" Black asked.

"Yes, sir."

Black took some money from his pocket and told Clint, "This'll be on me, since you're ridin' along to help me."

"Whatever you say."

Black paid, and they each carried a gunny sack out to their horse and tied it to their saddle.

"Butte?" Clint said to Black.

"Butte," Black agreed, and they rode out of town.

***

The first night they camped and split the chores. Clint saw to the horses while Black built the fire. They supped on jerky and beans, washed it down with coffee. They saved the canned peaches for another night.

They spent much of the day riding single file, so rather than conversation, they each spent a lot of time alone with their thoughts. It was only after they made camp and sat at the fire eating that they spoke.

"Tell me," Clint said, "are you sorry about what happened back at the saloon?"

"Those seven idiots called the play, Clint," Black said. "Sure, I'm sorry they're dead, but I'm glad as hell we ain't. You gonna tell me you feel different?"

Actually, Clint felt exactly the same, but there might have been a difference.

"No, you're right," he admitted, "I feel the same. I just wish there had been a different way to go."

"Next time, it might go different," Black said. "Don't think I don't know that you killed six of those seven. That's why I need your help. I know if it was just me and this Navy Colt, I'd be a dead man."

"As soon as we get to Butte, we'll find you a new gun," Clint said. "Most likely a Colt Peacemaker. Lighter, but deadly."

"What do we do to increase my speed?"

"That takes time," Clint said, "but I'm also interested in your accuracy. I've known a lot of lightning-fast gun artists who couldn't hit a thing once they got their guns out. It's often not the fastest, but the better marksman who endures."

"And where do your abilities stand?" Black asked. "You were fast as hell, back there. How accurate are you?"

"I don't miss," Clint admitted.

"Your aim is that good?"

"I never aim," Clint said. "I point and shoot. I can hit anything I point at."

"That's somethin' I'd like to see," Clay Black said.

"Tomorrow, at first light," Clint promised, "we'll do some shooting. How are you with a rifle?"

"Pretty good," Black said. "At least, I always thought so. I have the feelin' that shootin' with you is gonna change my mind."

"We'll see," Clint said.

With no reason for either of them to be on watch, they both turned in.

***

In the morning, Clint made a pot of coffee, beans and bacon for breakfast. When they were finished eating, he cleaned up, stowed away the pot and the pan, then turned to Black.

"Let's do some shooting," he said.

"That suits me," Black said, touching his gun,

Clint took the empty bean can and set it atop a boulder that was about fifty feet away.

"Think you can hit that?" Clint asked.

"No problem."

Black drew his Navy Colt and sighted down the barrel.

"I want you to do it without aiming," Clint said. "Just draw and fire."

Black looked apprehensive, but said, "All right," and holstered the gun.

"When I say 'now'," Clint said. He waited a few moments, then snapped, "Now!"

Clay Black drew, fired, and missed.

"I can see we've got some work to do," Clint said.

Chapter Fifteen

Clint had Black try a few more times, then said, "Give me that gun."

He took the Navy Colt and handed Black his modified Peacemaker.

"Now try with this," he said. "It's double-action, so you don't have to cock the hammer first."

Black took the gun and slid it into his holster, then lifted it and let it drop back in.

"It's lighter."

"Yes, it is," Clint said. "Give it a try."

Black turned to face the bean can, which had no holes in it, yet.

"Now!" Clint snapped.

Black drew and fired. The bullet struck the boulder just below the can, which knocked it to the ground without striking it.

"That was better. How did it feel?"

Black dropped the Colt back into his holster.

"It felt odd," he admitted. "But I drew faster, didn't I?"

"You seemed to," Clint said, "but we can concentrate on that later." He walked to the boulder, set the can back up on it and walked back.

"Forget about speed," he said. "I just want you to draw and fire and hit the can."

"Still without aimin'?"

"Yes."

Black tried to relax himself, then drew the Colt and fired. The can leaped into the air.

"Good," Clint said. "Now let's try a rifle."

He took his Colt back and returned the Navy Colt to Black. "Just to keep you balanced," he said.

Clint handed Clay Black his own rifle.

"Wait," Black said. "You said you'd show me how you shoot. That stuff about just pointing."

Clint drew, turned and fired. The empty can flew into the air, but before it could touch down he fired several more times, keeping the can jumping in the air. When it finally landed, it was a bullet-riddled mess.

"Damn!" Black said.

***

After a morning of shooting, they mounted up and started to ride. This time they kept pace, side-by-side, and Clint continued his lessons, speaking to Black about guns, and the proper ways to handle them.

"I always thought," Clay Black said, at one point, "that all you did was draw and fire. I didn't realize there was so much else involved."

"Distance, elevation, wind," Clint said, "it's all important as far as accuracy is concerned."

"When do we get to speed?" Black asked.

"Eventually," Clint said. "First let's buy you a new gun, and get you used to it."

"I feel like a kid learnin' to shoot, again," Black said.

"You do have to learn all over again," Clint said. "We have to deal with a lifetime of bad habits."

"What about fannin' the gun, like you did?"

"When you fan a gun that way, you jerk the barrel up every time your palm hits the hammer," Clint said. "That means you have to be aware of it each time, and force that barrel to stay down. It takes just the right amount of pressure, both ways. That's why I rarely do it, unless I think it's really necessary."

"Well, it sure did the job in that saloon," Clay Black observed.

They camped again the second night, figuring to make Butte the next afternoon. They supped again on beans and coffee, then made a second pot of coffee and sat at the fire, drinking it and swapping stories. Clayton

Black talked about some of the outlaws he had ridden with, while Clint discussed experiences with Wyatt Earp and Bat Masterson.

"Lemme ask you a quick question, Adams," Black said, eventually.

"Go ahead."

"You never once thought about walking on the other side of the law?"

"I've never had the urge to take something that wasn't mine," Clint said, "just because I wanted it."

"But as good as you are with a gun," Black said, "you could do that."

"Like I said," Clint repeated, "I've just never felt the urge."

"Never felt it," Black asked, "or never gave in."

"Never experienced it," Clint said.

Clayton Black looked as if this was something he just couldn't understand.

As they turned in, Clint realized that he didn't understand what drove Clayton Black to give in to the urge to steal what wasn't his.

Chapter Sixteen

They rode into Butte the next day and registered at the Homestead Hotel. They each got their own room and stowed their gear. Once that was done, they left the hotel to find a place to eat. The hotel dining room seemed to be set up only for breakfast.

As they sat across from each other eating steaks Clint said, "After this we can find a gunsmith's shop."

"Why do we need a gunsmith, we have you?" Black asked.

"I'll need to borrow his tools," Clint said. "The days when I used to travel around with mine are long gone."

"You actually were a traveling gunsmith?"

Clint nodded.

"Wagon, team, tools, the whole lot. Gave it up when I realized people would rather take a shot at me than have me work on their guns."

"But you haven't lost your touch?"

"Not at all," Clint said.

"But why do you need tools?" Black asked. "I thought we were just going to buy me a new gun."

"When I do buy you a new weapon, I'll have to tailor it to your touch. And I have an idea for a new holster."

"Sounds interestin'," Black said.

They finished their meals and hit the streets of Butte, looking for a gunshop or a gunsmith's shop. It took several streets, but they finally came upon the complete package. A sign in the window said GUNS FOR SALE! GUNS REPAIRED!

They entered, and Clint immediately saw the difference between this store and the junk shop in Tylerville. All the weapons hanging on the walls or laid out on shelves were clean and new. The gray-haired man behind the counter was busy with a pistol that was in pieces. He was bent over it, peering through a pair of wire-framed glasses perched on the edge of his bulbous nose. When they approached the counter, he looked up at them over the frames.

"Help ya?" he asked.

"We're looking for a gun," Clint said.

"I got plenty."

"I can see that," Clint said. "We'd just like to look around for a while, if you don't mind."

"Help yerself," the man said. "Most of my stock is new, but on that back wall you'll find some rebuilt guns that are a might cheaper."

"Thanks."

Clint turned to Black and said, "Let's look around."

They walked along the walls, where pistols hung on pegs by their trigger guards.

"What about this one?" Black asked, pointing to a silver pistol.

"We don't want anything too flashy, or too new," Clint said.

"Why not too new?"

"It'll be unproven," Clint explained. "You never know if and when a new model is going to jam."

Black replaced the revolver, and they continued to look. The next one he plucked off the wall was a Remington Rider Double-action Belt Revolver.

"This feels good in my hand," Black said.

"That's because it's a replacement for that old Navy Colt you're carrying. It has a smaller frame and shorter barrel, but still carries the six shot, thirty-six caliber cylinder."

Black hefted the gun in his hand and said, "I like the weight."

"Give me that Navy Colt," Clint said. "Put that in your holster"

He handed Clint the older, clunkier gun and put the new stream-lined model into his holster.

"How's it feel?" Clint asked.

"Good," Black said, "it feels good."

"Let me see it."

Black took the gun out and handed it to Clint. He spun the cylinder and worked the action, hefted it.

"This'll do," he said, "depending on how you can shoot with it."

"What about the holster?"

"That," Clint said, "I'll have to make, or have this fellow make. Let's see."

They went to the counter, where the old-timer was waiting.

"Found something you like?"

"I think so," Clint said, setting the gun down on the countertop.

"This gun ain't gonna last," the man said. "It can't compete with the Peacemaker."

"I like it," Black said.

The old man shrugged.

"To each his own."

"We'll need a couple of boxes of shells," Clint said.

"Plannin' a war?" the man asked.

"Just a lot of practice," Clint said.

The man set the boxes of shells on the countertop next to the gun.

"Anythin' else?"

"Yes," Clint said, "I have an idea for a holster . . ."

Chapter Seventeen

They left the shop with the gun. The gunsmith, whose name was Darrow, said the holster would take some time.

"We'll be back," Clint said.

"Whose name should I put on the order?" Darrow asked.

"Adams, Clint Adams."

Darrow looked shocked.

"In that case, I'll have it in two days."

Outside the shop, Black put his hand on the Remington in his holster. They had left the Navy Colt with Darrow.

"What now?" Black asked.

"We need a place to do some shooting," Clint said.

Black grinned.

"Why not right here?" he asked.

"No," Clint said, "not on the street. Not in town. We'll ride out and find a clearing, take a few targets with us."

"What kind of targets?"

"That café we ate in," Clint said. "I'm sure they have empty cans and bottles we can use."

"Then we'll need some sacks," Black said. "That means the general store."

"You go and get us a couple of gunny sacks and meet me at the café," Clint said. "Then we'll ride out and find a clearing."

"Right."

They separated.

***

Clint went to the café and got the waiter's attention.

"Empty bottles and cans?" the waiter said. "Yes, we have many."

"Good, I need them," Clint said. "I can buy them from you."

The man waved his hand.

"No need," he said. "Givin' them to you means we don't have to throw them away ourselves. Do you have somethin' to carry them in?"

"I will," Clint said. "I have a man coming with some gunny sacks."

"Good," the waiter said. "When he gets here, I'll fill them for you."

It was only a few minutes before Clay Black walked in with the sacks. They gave them to the waiter, who took them into the kitchen and filled them both. He brought them out, bulging.

"Cans," he said, holding one up, "and bottles."

"Thank you," Clint said, taking one sack while Black took the other. "Now the livery, for our horses," Clint said.

***

They rode out of town and, just to the east, found a likely clearing.

Clint set up the cans and bottles on top of rocks and boulders, then stepped back to stand alongside Clay Black.

"Don't worry about speed, now," he said. "Just hit the targets."

Black drew and fired six times, striking two cans and a bottle.

"I still feel like I have to aim," he said, as he reloaded.

"You'll get over that," Clint said. "The barrel of the gun is an extension of your forefinger. All you have to do is point with confidence, and you'll hit what you're pointing at. Let's go again."

This time Black fired six times and hit two cans and two bottles.

"Again!"

Black reloaded and fired again. This time he missed once.

"Let's keep going until you don't miss," Clint said.

They went through a box of shells, but eventually Black was hitting the targets six out of six times.

"Not bad, huh?" Black asked, reloading.

"Not bad, at all," Clint said. "In the next few days, we can work on speed, as soon as we get the new holster."

"What's gonna be so special about this new one?"

"You'll see," Clint said. "Let's get back to town. I'm ready to eat again."

"So am I."

***

When they got back to town, they went to the same café, where the waiter greeted them with a smile.

"How did the cans and the bottles do, gents?" he asked.

"They were perfect," Clint said.

He showed them to a back table. There were more people at the other tables than there had been earlier, but nobody seemed to be paying any attention to them.

"Gents?" the waiter said.

"Steak," Black said.

"Two," Clint said.

"Comin' up."

He brought Clay Black a beer and Clint a pot of coffee.

"I'm sure glad we ran into each other in Tylerville," Black said. "I can see the difference, already."

"And as the days go by, you'll see an even bigger difference," Clint said.

"You know," Black said, "you probably have extended not only my life by a few years, but my career, as well."

His career? Clint thought. As an outlaw?

Chapter Eighteen

After they ate, Black said he was going to look for a saloon. Clint decided not to go with the man. The two of them together might be too much of a temptation for trouble. Also, he had some thinking to do. He knew he was probably helping Clay Black stay alive a bit longer by increasing his dexterity with a gun. But his intention was not to extend the man's life as an outlaw. He was starting to think he might have made a mistake by agreeing to help him. But neither did he feel he could back out, now.

Black had the room right across the hall from Clint's, so he heard him return a couple of hours later. He listened for the door to Black's room to open, but instead there was a knock at his own door. Gun in hand, he went to the door.

"Clay?"

"It's me."

He opened the door. Clay Black stood a bit unsteady in the hall.

"Is anything wrong?" Clint asked. "Did something happen?"

"No, no," Black said. "I just wanted you to know I was back."

"So, no trouble?"

"Believe it or not, Clint," Black said. "I try to avoid trouble."

"That's good."

"Especially in a territory where I'm not already wanted. Good-night."

"See you for breakfast," Clint said, "and then we'll get back to shooting."

"That's okay with me."

Black left, closing the door behind him. Moments later Clint heard the door to the room across the hall open and close.

***

The next morning, they had breakfast in the hotel dining room. While they ate, they talked about shooting. Clint gave Black some more tips about handling a gun and keeping it in working order.

"You've got to break it down, clean it and oil it as often as you can," Clint said. "The last thing you need is a gun jamming on you when you really need it."

75

"That happened to me a few times with the Navy Colt," Black admitted. "Luckily, at the time I was ridin' with good men who had my back."

"Where are they now?" Clint asked.

"Dead," Black said. "They're all dead. Yeah, that's another reason I decided to spend some time where I ain't wanted. I gotta figure out where I'm gonna get some more good men." He looked up from his plate at Clint. "I don't suppose . . ."

"No," Clint said, "I'm still not ready to ride the outlaw trail. Sorry."

"Ah, that's okay," Black said. "I didn't really expect you to say yes. Besides, you're doin' your part by keepin' me alive."

"So you're going back to . . . what? Robbing trains? Stagecoaches?"

"Wherever the money is," Black said.

"I can't help feeling I'll be helping you."

"Like I said," Black commented, "you're helpin' me stay alive. What I do with my life's got nothin' to do with you. Whether we met or not, I'd still be robbin' trains."

"You said the railroads were behind the high price on your head?"

"It's all a game, Clint," he said. "I hit as many trains as I can, and they keep sendin' bounty hunters and detectives after me."

"Pinkertons?"

"Among others," Black said.

"And do they all know it's a game?"

"Guess not," Black said. "That's probably why I play it better than most."

Clint didn't think much of dodging the law and trying to stay alive as a game.

***

After breakfast they got their horses from the livery and rode back out to their clearing. The bottles and cans were still there. Once again Clint had Black fire the gun until he was hitting six out of six targets.

"What's next?" Black asked.

"We're going to pick up that holster later today," Clint said, "but for now, let's see how good you are with your Winchester."

They fetched Black's rifle from his saddle.

"Now, this is a little different from firing a pistol," Clint said. "You're most likely further away, so with a rifle, you *will* be aiming."

Clint set up some bottles and cans, then paced off a hundred feet.

"When I say 'now,' lever and fire six times. Let's see how you do. Now!"

Chapter Nineteen

Clayton Black's ability with a rifle was acceptable. Most men who lived on the wrong side of the law depended on their pistol skills to stay alive. The rifle was more often than not used for hunting.

When Clint called a halt to the shooting, they headed back to town to pick up the new holster Clint had designed for Black.

Darrow was behind the counter, once again working on a weapon he'd broken down into pieces.

"How'd it go with that holster, Darrow?" Clint asked.

"I think you're gonna like what you see, Mr. Adams," the older man said. "It's in the back. Lemme get it for ya."

"I can't wait to see this," Black said.

"I think you'll be surprised."

Darrow came out of the backroom holding a rolled-up leather gunbelt. He took it with him to his side of the counter and then unfurled it.

"Strap it on," Clint told Black.

Black took the gunbelt, removed his old one, put the new one on, then put his hand down to the holster to insert his new gun.

"This feels odd," he said. "What's it made of?"

"Parkesine," Darrow said. "It's a substance that was discovered by a British fella named Alexander Parkes. It softens when heated, but when it cools it gets real hard."

"What's better about it?" Black asked Clint.

"Draw your gun," Clint said, "but don't lift it up, just grab it and swing your arm out."

Black frowned but reached for his gun, and before he knew it the holster had sprung open.

"What the—"

"It's on a hinge," Darrow said. "Then you set your gun back in and swing it shut. See? It locks in place until the next time you need it."

Black replaced the gun, then drew it again.

"That's fast," he said, in awe.

"You're getting a couple of seconds, now, with the new holster, and the double-action," Clint explained. "In a gunfight, all you need is that extra second or two."

Black replaced the gun and locked the holster in place.

"Just don't ever leave that holster in the sun," Darrow warned.

"Hang onto the old one," Clint said, "just in case you get stuck in the desert."

"I'm still tryin' to come up with somethin' that won't melt," Darrow said. "But that spring latch, that was Mr. Adams' idea."

"We'll try it out for real tomorrow," Clint said. "What do we owe you, Darrow?"

Darrow gave Clint what he thought was a reasonable price, and Clint agreed. It was Black, though, who took the money from his pocket and handed it to Darrow.

They left the gunsmith shop with Black carrying his old gunbelt over his shoulder.

"Supper?" Clint asked.

"Let's go by our hotel first. I wanna drop this old belt off in my room."

Clint agreed, and they headed for the hotel.

***

After dropping the holster off, they went to the café they had already eaten at a couple of times. The food was good, and they saw no reason to go looking elsewhere.

They both ordered a bowl of beef stew on the recommendation of the waiter. During the meal, Black kept letting his hand drop down by his new holster, feeling the smoothness of it.

"This gun and holster are both gonna take some gettin' used to."

"You will," Clint said. "Just give it some time."

"Once I do get used to them, I'll be able to leave Montana Territory," Black said. "Then I can recruit some new . . . partners."

"Are all your old ones gone?" Clint asked.

"Not all of them," Black said. "Unfortunately, some of them are lookin' for me. Another reason I came to Montana Territory."

"I'm assuming there was a difference of opinion between you and your partners."

"Oh yeah," Black said. "That pretty much always happens, unless you're the James boys."

"Believe me," Clint said, "Frank and Jesse didn't always see eye-to-eye."

"You knew them?"

"I did."

"So then you're used to havin' outlaws as friends."

"Not really," Clint said. "I think I was just sympathetic to the reasons they robbed trains."

Black laughed.

"You won't be sympathetic with my reasons," he said.

"And they are?"

"Simple," Black said, with a shrug. "I rob trains because I want to."

Chapter Twenty

"How many?" Clint asked.

"How many what?"

"How many partners are looking for you?"

Black shrugged.

"Two or three," he said, "unless they've joined up with others."

"Are they looking to kill you?"

"I'm sure they are," Black said. "But so are the bounty hunters."

"What about the detectives? And the law?"

"They just want to catch me," Black said.

"Why not stay in Montana and go straight?" Clint asked.

"I can't go straight, Clint," Black said, "any more than you can put down your gun. It's just too damn late, even if I wanted to, which I don't. I like my life."

"You know what happened to Jesse, don't you?"

Black nodded.

"Shot in the back by a relative," he said. "But he had gone straight when he was killed. You see? It didn't matter."

"I get your point."

They finished their meal off with coffee.

"What do we do now to pass the time til tomorrow?" Black asked.

"We stay indoors," Clint said, "and out of sight."

"I told you once before," Black said, "I don't wanna hide."

"Isn't that what you're doing here in Montana?" Clint asked. "Hiding?"

"Let's call it . . . reestablishing myself," Black said.

Clint remained silent.

"You're havin' a problem with helpin' me," Black said. "You think you made the wrong decision?"

"I may have," Clint said, "but I also made a commitment, which I intend to honor."

"Good!"

"I just don't want you to do anything to make me regret it," Clint added.

"Like what?" Black said. "I intend to do what I always do. And I'd do it whether you helped me or not."

"Rob all the trains you want," Clint said. "Just don't kill anybody."

"I told you when we first met," Black said. "I'm not a killer."

"So you said."

"And I meant it," Black said. "You won't see the words 'murder' or 'killer' next to my picture on any wanted poster in any state or territory."

"What about 'dead-or-alive'?" Clint asked. "That's usually reserved for killers."

"That's the railroads," Black said. "You can't imagine how many times I've stolen from them. They'll do anythin' to stop me. But look, I don't ever apologize for who I am, or what I've done. If you can't accept that, I understand." Black smiled. "We can shake hands and go our separate ways."

Now Clint understood what it was he saw in Clayton Black. He reminded him of his late, good friend, Wild Bill Hickok. James Butler Hickok never apologized for who he was and what he did. They were friends even though Clint knew that Hickok—a famed lawman—had also spent some time on the other side of the law, when he felt he had to. The philosophy of Clayton Black seemed the same.

"Like I told you before, Clay," Clint said. "I honor my commitments. So we'll see this through, and then we'll go our own ways."

"Deal!" Black said.

The two men paid their bill, left the café and went back to their hotel.

***

Clint sat in his room, wondering if he was mellowing because he was getting older. But as far as he knew, Clayton Black wasn't known as a killer, just an outlaw. Clint had outlaw friends before, not the least of which were the James boys. But he didn't know much about Clay Black, except that he reminded him of Jim Hickok.

When their association was done, he certainly wouldn't call Black his friend.

***

Clayton Black sat in his room, slid his new gun from his equally new holster and fondled it. He had gotten exactly what he wanted—no, needed—from Clint Adams. His new ability with a gun was going to come in very handy when he returned to the Southwest.

He had told Clint Adams the truth. There were three ex-partners who were looking for him. He knew he was going to need an edge when they found him, and now he had it, thanks to the Gunsmith.

***

The next day they went to their makeshift shooting range and Clint put Black through his paces with his pistol, and his rifle.

"Not bad," Clint said. "Now, let's try drawing."

Black put the gun back in the holster.

"All right, when I say now, draw and fire, just once. I want you to hit the bottle on the right. Now!"

Black drew and fired. The bottle shattered.

"Good," Clint said. "Now do it faster. The bottle on the left. Ready? Now!"

Black drew and fired. Again, the bottle shattered.

"How was that?" Black asked.

"How did it feel?" Clint asked.

"Good," Black said, "Fast."

"Then I think we're done here," Clint said. "All you need to do is keep practicing. You'll only get better."

"I owe you a lot," Black said. "I could pay you—"

Clint put his hand up to cut the man off. Although he might need to use the money, he wouldn't feel right accepting it. He still wasn't sure he'd done the right thing, to begin with.

"No payment's necessary."

"Well then," Black said, "I'll be leavin' town as soon as we get back."

Chapter Twenty-One

Three months later . . .

Her name was Elizabeth Green, and in the town of Chandler, Arizona, she was the postmistress.

Clint met Liz when he went to the post office, which was in the mercantile. He was waiting for a letter and wanted to let them know he was in town. Expecting a male postmaster, he was stunned to find her behind the counter. She was tall, slender, extremely elegant looking, her hair pinned up on her head, showing off a long, graceful neck.

"I was looking for the postmaster," he said.

"I'm the postmistress," she told him. "Can I help you?"

"Do you have a letter for me?" he asked. "My name's Clint Adams."

She turned and looked at an empty slot behind her.

"No, Sir, I'm sorry," she said. "Nothing yet."

"Well," he said, "I'll be at the Colonial Hotel."

"If it arrives," she said, "I'll send a message."

"Would you be bringing that message yourself?" he asked.

She smiled.

"I'm sure I can find someone to run it over to you."

"I'm new in town," he said, "and I need someone to tell me a good place to eat. Maybe you could show me?"

"Mr. Adams, is it?"

"That's right."

"Do you often invite women to dinner the first time you meet them?"

"Never," he told her. "That should show you how desperate I am for company."

"I'm sure I can direct you to a good restaurant."

"This town is growing," he said. "I might get lost."

"You're quite persistent, aren't you?"

"Sometimes," he said. "This happens to be one of those times."

"Well . . . let's see what happens when that letter arrives," she suggested.

"I'll take that as a firm maybe, Miss Green." He had read her name on a plaque on the wall.

"If you'll excuse me," she said, "I have some work to do."

"Yes, Ma'am."

He left the mercantile, hoping he had made a good impression on the lady.

***

A telegram had caught up to Clint in a town called Hopkins, Nevada, asking him to come to Chandler, Arizona, where a letter would be waiting for him. The telegram also assured him that it would be worth his while.

Since he had nowhere else to be, he decided to make the ride to Chandler and check it out. So, he was sitting in a chair in front of his hotel, hoping against hope that when the letter did arrive the postmistress herself would bring it to him.

Before stopping at the mercantile, however, he had stopped into the sheriff's office to announce his arrival. He had found a young deputy there, told him who he was and what hotel he would be at. So, he wasn't surprised to see a man with a badge walking toward him.

"Mr. Adams?" the man asked when he reached Clint.

"How did you know?"

"I guessed," the man said. "You're a stranger. My name is Sheriff Morgan. My deputy told me you dropped in."

"I like to check in with the local law when I arrive in a town," Clint said. "It avoids any surprises."

"I appreciate that," Morgan said. He was a tall, rangy man of about forty or so. His manner did not give any indication of nerves in talking with the Gunsmith. Clint liked that.

"Mind tellin' me what you're doin' in Chandler?" the lawman asked.

"Not at all," Clint said. "I'm waiting for a letter."

"Here?" Morgan asked. "In front of the hotel?"

"I stopped into your post office, but it wasn't there, yet," Clint said. "I told the postmistress I'd be here."

"Ah, our Miss Green," Morgan said.

"Yes," Clint said, "I expected a man, but she seems competent enough."

"More than competent," Morgan said. "She's highly thought of in town."

"That's good to know," Clint said.

"Um, a fella like you is takin' a chance, sittin' out here in the open like this."

"A fella like me takes a chance waking up in the morning, Sheriff," Clint said. "I can't start hiding, not at this age."

"I suppose not," Morgan said. "I just don't want anybody recognizing you and taking a potshot at you."

"You and me both."

"Well," the lawman said, "thanks for checkin' in with us, and I'd appreciate you lettin' us know when you're leavin' town."

"I'll do that, Sheriff."

"Good day to you," the lawman said, and walked away, leaving Clint impressed by the man. So far, he liked the two people in town he had spoken with for more than five minutes: Sheriff Morgan, and postmistress Elizabeth Green.

Chapter Twenty-Two

Clint was pleasantly surprised when Elizabeth Green appeared, crossing the street toward him. He started to stand as she came closer.

"Oh, please don't get up," she said. "In fact, do you mind if I sit next to you?"

"Not at all." He reached over and pulled another chair closer to him, and she sat.

"Here you are," she said, holding something out to him. "Your letter."

"Oh, it came," he said accepting it.

"Actually, it was there the whole time," she said. "It was in the wrong slot.

"I suppose that happens quite a bit," he said.

"It's not supposed to," she said. "Please, don't tell anyone. I don't want to lose my job."

"I'll tell you what," he said. "If you'll have dinner with me tonight, I won't tell."

"Well," she said, "I was just on my way home and thought I'd drop off your letter. Why don't you let me change my clothes, and then fetch me at my house. I can take you to a good place to eat."

"That sounds great."

She stood and gave him directions to her house, which was inside the town limits.

"It's a small house they gave me to go with the job," she said. "Say, in an hour?"

"I'll be there," he said.

"I'm looking forward to it."

He watched her cross back to the other side of the street, and then stroll away, exchanging greetings with people as she passed them.

He stood up, went into the hotel and up to his room. Once there he examined the letter. There was no return address. His name had been written in an almost unreadable scrawl.

Finally, he slit the envelope open and took out the letter. It was written in the same scrawl. As he unfolded it, a hundred-dollar bill fluttered to the floor.

He picked up the bill, then looked at the letter. It said: NOW THAT YOU ARE IN ARIZONA, LOOK FOR CLAYTON BLACK.

Clint hadn't thought about Clay Black in three months. During that time, he hadn't heard or read anything about the man.

Whoever sent the letter, and the hundred-dollar bill, wanted Clint to find Black. But why?

He refolded the letter, put it and the hundred-dollar bill back in the envelope, then put the envelope into his saddlebag. He didn't want to think about Clay Black now. He wanted to think about Elizabeth Green.

***

Clint followed Elizabeth Green's directions to a small, well-appointed house, with a white picket fence around it. He went up the walk to the front door and knocked. When she answered he was struck momentarily dumb.

"Hello," she said, "Mr. Adams, right?"

"Clint," he said. "You look lovely."

Her hair was down, hanging past her shoulders, and her glasses were gone. Her eyes were a violet color, and gleaming.

"Thank you," she said. "I'm ready to take you to a nice restaurant."

"Good," he said. "I'm ready to eat in one."

As they walked away from the house, she slid her arm through his left.

Chapter Twenty-Three

She took him to a steak house in the center of town. The way she was greeted, it was obvious she ate there quite often. When Clint asked for a back table, his request was happily granted. As they walked past the other tables, people greeted their postmistress with smiles.

"You seem very popular," Clint said, as they sat.

"All you have to do is make sure people get their mail," she said. "Speaking of which, was your letter important?"

"As it turns out, not very," Clint said. "But maybe it was just a way for me to meet you."

"You have a way with words, Mr. Adams," she said. "I thought your way was with a gun."

"I can do either, when the time comes," Clint said.

"Would you mind if I ordered for both of us?"

"Not at all," he said. "This is your place."

The meal was excellent, the conversation was even better, and eventually when Clint walked her home, she invited him inside.

"I have a special delivery for you," she told him. "That is, if my boldness isn't frightening you."

She took him to her bedroom, and he watched as she undressed. She was long and lean, but her breasts—though small—seemed very firm. Her skin was incredibly smooth, and between her legs her bush was darker than the hair on her head, a curtain that he knew, when parted, would lead to something special.

"Are you going to undress for me?" she asked.

"I am."

"Slowly?"

"If that's what you want?"

She laughed, deep in her throat, and sat on the bed, leaning back on her hands.

"That's what I want."

He started to unbutton his shirt.

"Wait! Wait!" she said, suddenly.

He stopped.

She went to the oil lamp on the night table and turned it down to a soft glow, then sat back down on the bed.

"Now."

He undid his gunbelt and set it down within reach, then went back to the buttons on his shirt. He undressed slowly, as she asked, and when his hard cock came into view she smiled widely.

"I knew it," she said. "Come here."

He walked to the bed, and she put her arms around him, dug her nails into his buttocks and pulled him to her so that his penis was between her breasts. The heat of her skin burned him, even though his cock was also hot.

She kissed his chest, then pushed him away so she could sink to her knees in front of him. She took his hard cock into her hot mouth and sucked him until the length of him was gleaming with her saliva. Then she stood, got back on the bed, pulled him with her and urged him to fuck her.

He mounted her as she lay on her back and drove himself into her. He pounded away, again and again, administering his own special delivery . . .

***

In another part of Arizona, Clayton Black sat in a saloon with two men, sharing a bottle of whiskey.

"I don't get it," Slim Jackson said. "Why send him a letter?"

"I want him to find me, Slim," Black said.

"Why?"

"I've killed three men in the past three months," Black said. "Three men who might've killed me if the Gunsmith hadn't helped me."

"That's why you want him to find you?" the other man, Jess Fuller, asked. "To thank him?"

"You could say that," Clay Black said. "But I also wanna show him what he did, how successful he was in helping me stay alive."

"And the three men you killed?"

"Old partners," he said.

"You always kill your partner?" Jackson asked, looking worried.

"Only if they turn on me," Black sad, "and these three did."

"And now they're dead," Jackson said.

"That's right," Black said. "I killed all three of them, one-by-one, face-to-face. And when Clint Adams hears about it, he'll come lookin'."

"How sure are you he'll hear about it?" Fuller asked.

"Dead sure," Black said.

"And what are you gonna do when the Gunsmith finds you?" Jackson asked.

"I'm gonna use the same skills he helped me develop," Black said. "To kill him, fair and square, right in the middle of the street."

"You're gonna kill the Gunsmith?" Jackson said.

Clayton Black poured himself a drink and said, "You bet."

Chapter Twenty-Four

Three days after he arrived and read the first letter, a second one came.

When Liz Green and Clint had dinner together for the third night in a row, she handed him the envelope across the table.

"This arrived today," she said.

Across the front was the same handwriting.

"Aren't you going to open it?" she asked.

"Later," he said. "For now, I want to know how your day went."

"Boring," she said. "My job is boring. I was hoping your letter might perk my day up, somewhat."

"All right," he said, slitting the envelope, "let's see if we can do that."

There was no hundred-dollar bill, this time. Instead of a letter, there was simply one line scrawled on a slip of paper. It said: YOU DID A GOOD JOB. And there was a newspaper clipping.

"What's that?" she asked.

He looked at it. It was from a newspaper called the *Arizona Chronicle*. MAN SHOT DEAD IN THE STREET BY CLAYTON BLACK. He handed it to Liz.

"What's it mean?" she asked.

"It means someone wants me to know that Clay Black killed a man."

"And who is Clay Black?"

"An outlaw," Clint said.

"And you know him?"

"I do."

"How?"

"I helped him once."

"You helped an outlaw?"

"Oh, I didn't help him break the law," Clint said. He explained the short relationship he'd had with Clayton Black.

"Then you don't have anything to be sorry for," she reasoned.

"I didn't think so," Clint said, "but somebody wants me to know about this."

"Did your other letter have something to do with this, as well?" she asked.

"Yes," he said. "It suggested that I should probably go looking for Clay Black."

"And will you?"

"No," he said, taking the clipping back and folding it up, again. "I have the feeling this isn't the last envelope I'll be receiving here."

"So that means you'll be staying in town a bit longer," she said.

"I guess it does."

"Then I'll be on the lookout for another envelope," she said.

***

The next day—after another energetic night with Liz Green—Clint decided to stop in on Sheriff Morgan. This time he found the man in his office, seated at his desk, which was off to the side, beneath a rifle rack.

"Ah, Mr. Adams" Morgan said. "Come to tell me you're leavin'?"

"I'm afraid not, Sheriff," Clint said. "Do you know anything about this?" He handed the lawman the newspaper clipping.

Morgan read it and handed it back.

"I know who Clayton Black is, of course," he said. "He's a wanted man in Arizona and a few other states and territories. What's this got to do with you staying in town?"

"Somebody sent me this in the mail," Clint said.

"Why?"

"All I can figure is that they wanted me to know about it," Clint said.

"Well, according to the date on that clipping, it happened months ago."

"I didn't know about it."

"Then you don't know about the other two?"

"What other two?"

"Have a seat, Mr. Adams," Morgan said, and Clint did. "Since killin' that man, Black has killed two more."

"The same way?" Clint asked.

Morgan nodded.

"Face-to-face in the street. They say Black is lightning fast."

"I'm afraid that's my fault."

Clint remembered that Black said there were some ex-partners after him. Apparently, he had managed to deal with them.

"How so?"

Briefly, Clint explained the situation to Morgan.

"Well," Morgan said, "I can't say I understand why you would do that, but it doesn't mean it's your fault he decided to kill his partners in that way."

"Isn't it?"

"What do you intend to do about it?"

"Somebody wants me to know these things," Clint said. "I suspect I'll be getting two more clippings in the mail. I'll wait for them before I decide what to do."

"You think you're gonna end up trackin' him down?" Morgan asked.

Clint stood up.

"I'm taking a wait-and-see attitude."

Chapter Twenty-Five

It was several days later when the third envelope arrived. Clint had been thinking about leaving town instead of waiting any longer, but Liz came by the hotel with the latest one.

He opened the door to his room and let her in. She handed him the envelope.

"Thanks for bringing it over," he said, opening it.

"Anything different?" she asked.

"This time there's no note," he said, "just a clipping from the same newspaper about the second shooting."

"Did it happen in the same place?"

"No," Clint said, "this one took place in a small town called Ashford. I never heard of it."

"So now what?" she asked.

"According to Sheriff Morgan, there's been three shootings," Clint told her. "I might as well wait for the third clipping."

"And then what?"

"I don't know," he said. "I'll decide when the time comes."

"Well," she said, "I have to get back to work."

"One thing," he said.

"Yes?"

"Can you tell where these were mailed from?"

"No," she said. "Whoever it is has been very careful not to list a return address. And this is odd. There's no post mark. It's as if these envelopes have been hand-delivered."

"Okay," he said, "thanks."

"Dinner tonight?" she asked.

"Sure, but is there someplace different we can eat?" he asked.

"There sure is," she said. "My house. Come by at seven. I'll cook."

"Can you cook?" he asked.

She laughed.

"You're gonna find out."

She left and he sat on the bed with the two clippings. Who was sending them, along with a hundred-dollar bill? It didn't seem the kind of thing Clayton Black would do, but then Clint really didn't know the man that well. Of course, it could have been someone totally different, but who knew the story about Clint tutoring Black with a gun? Perhaps a reporter? He looked at the byline on the clippings and decided that after the third one came, he would visit the office of the *Arizona Chronicle* and see how much David Kellogg knew.

***

He appeared at Liz Green's door at seven sharp.

She kissed him and said, "Come on in. Dinner's almost ready. I hope you like chicken."

"It's my second favorite after steak," he said.

"Well, you've had steak the past three nights. I thought it was time for something different."

"That suits me," he assured her.

When they reached the sitting room of the small house, she handed him a glass of white wine.

"I know you prefer beer," she said, "but I'm trying to set a mood."

"Wine's okay," he said.

"Good. Have a seat, drink your wine, and I'll call you when dinner is served."

"It smells great," he told her.

"That's a good start," she said, and hurried into the kitchen.

He sat on her sofa making himself comfortable and sipped the wine. He was still thinking about Clayton Black and the men he had killed when she called out, "dinner's ready!"

As it turned out, she was a very good cook. The chicken was succulent, and the vegetables perfectly done. They had more wine with dinner.

"I found something for you, today," she said, as they were finishing.

"What's that?"

"Let me clean up here, and I'll bring it to you."

He went back to the sofa to wait, and when she entered, she handed him a newspaper.

"It's the *Arizona Chronicle*," she said. "I thought it might be helpful for you to know where this paper came from."

"You're brilliant," he said, accepting it. "That was one of the things I was going to investigate."

"That's not one of the editions the clippings came from," she said, "but at least you now know the paper originates from Tucson."

"It's been a while since I've been to Tucson," he said. "I'll bet it's grown quite a bit."

"I also sent a telegram to the post office in Tucson, to see if the envelopes were mailed from there."

"And?"

"They couldn't tell me."

"That's all right," he said. "I appreciate the effort."

"Well then," she said, "maybe now you can show me some effort."

They each carried a glass of wine to the bedroom.

Chapter Twenty-Six

The next envelope came several days later. Once again, a newspaper clipping and a note saying THAT MAKES THREE, THANKS TO YOU.

He opened it while standing in front of Liz Green's desk in the mercantile.

"Now what will you do?" she asked.

Tucking the envelope into his pocket he said, "I have to decide if this is the last one."

"And if it is?"

"Then I'm heading to Tucson."

"When will you know?"

"If another envelope doesn't come by the end of the week," he said. "I'll just figure there isn't going to be another one, and it'll be time for me to go."

"Then you'll be looking for Clayton Black?"

"First, I'll want to find out what this newspaper fellow, Kellogg, knows. Maybe he's even the one sending me the clippings."

"And if he is?"

"If he is," Clint said, "he's going to tell me why."

***

By the end of the week there was no more mail. Clint saddled his Tobiano and rode over to the sheriff's office. He had already said goodbye to Liz.

As he entered the office, the sheriff and his deputy turned and looked at him.

"Go and make your rounds, Travis," Morgan said, and the young deputy left. "Mr. Adams, what brings you here?"

"You said you wanted to know when I was leaving," Clint said. "Well, I'm leaving."

"I have to say," Morgan said, "I didn't much notice that you were here."

"I like to stay out of trouble."

"I'm sure that's not always easy for a man with your reputation," Morgan said, "but I'm obliged to you. Where are you off to?"

"Tucson," Clint said, "then . . . who knows?"

"Well, good luck to you," Morgan said, "wherever you end up."

"Thanks."

Clint left the office, mounted Toby, and rode out of town.

***

He camped on the trail two nights before reaching Tucson.

Clint knew that Morgan Earp had been killed in Tucson, and the town was the starting point for Wyatt Earp's ride for vengeance, where he tracked down and killed, among others, Frank Stilwell. It had a long and wild history, but as he rode into town, he could tell it was far from a wild, frontier town now. In fact, he rode past the University of Arizona, which had been opened only a year or so ago. It made sense that a newspaper like the *Arizona Chronicle* would be based in Tucson.

He registered at The Palace Hotel and took his horse to a livery stable. Then he wasted no time. With his saddlebags over his shoulder and rifle in hand, he went in search of the newspaper office.

He found it and entered. The sound of the press was deafening, as an older man with an ink-stained white apron ran it. When the man saw Clint he stopped, and the silence was almost as deafening.

"Help ya?" he asked.

"I'm looking for David Kellogg."

"He's the editor," the man said. "Back office, right through there." He pointed to a doorway.

"Thanks," Clint said.

The doorway led him to a long hallway, with another door at the end of it. When he reached the door, he knocked on the frosted glass window upon which was etched DAVID KELLOGG, EDITOR.

"Come in!"

Clint entered. The man was sitting at his desk with his back to the door. He turned in his chair and stared at Clint. He appeared to be about forty, perhaps twenty years younger than the man running the press.

"What can I do for you?"

"I have some questions for you," Clint said. "My name's Clint Adams."

"Jesus!" Kellogg said. "Let me get my pad. Are you here for an interview?"

"I don't do interviews, Mr. Kellogg."

The man stopped looking for his pad.

"Then why are you here?"

Clint took the three clippings from his pocket and handed them to Kellogg.

"Somebody sent me these in the mail," Clint said, "one at a time. Was it you?"

Kellogg took the clippings, examined them and handed them back.

"It wasn't me," he said. "I wrote them, but I never sent them to you."

"Any idea who did?" Clint asked.

"Now how would I know that?" the editor asked.

"I guess you wouldn't," Clint said, and turned to leave.

"Hey!" Kellogg yelled. "Are you sure about that interview?"

"Positive," Clint tossed over his shoulder.

Chapter Twenty-Seven

Clint went to his hotel to clean up and consider his next move. He'd been hoping for better luck with the newspaper editor.

The room had modern amenities, including a water closet where he could pump water into a sink, and run his own bath, if he wanted to.

He removed his dirty shirt, got cleaned up in the sink, and donned a fresh one. He moved the three clippings to a new pocket, although he wasn't sure what he was going to do with them.

He decided to fill his rumbling belly while continuing to figure out his next move. The Palace had a large dining room, so there was no point in looking elsewhere. He got a back table and studied the impressive menu, which had not only the normal American dishes but also selections from other countries. He stayed with his favorite, though, and just ordered a steak dinner. He didn't want to spend a lot of time thinking about food. He had other things on his mind.

While he ate, he decided the best thing to do next was check in with the local law. Tucson being the big town it was, he assumed they'd not only have a sheriff but a more modern police department.

To determine where he should go first, he stopped at the front desk after leaving the dining room.

"Yes, sir," the clerk said, "we do have a sheriff and a police department."

"Can you direct me to both?"

"Of course."

The clerk gave him directions, and Clint decided to go to the sheriff's office first, which was closest to the hotel.

It was an easy walk, and when he reached the office, he knocked before entering.

"Not too many people do that," the man behind the desk said.

"What's that?" Clint asked.

"Knock before comin' into my office," the lawman said, "but then, it's probably because you're a stranger in town."

"You got that right," Clint said. "I just arrived to-day."

"Then you probably don't know we got a spankin' brand new police department," the sheriff said.

"I do know that, Sheriff," Clint said. "I chose to come here first."

"Well," the man said. "I'm Sheriff Gabe Hynes. Who're you, young fella."

The sheriff was in his sixties, which was why he was able to refer to Clint as "young fella."

"My name's Clint Adams."

The sheriff sat back and folded his arms across his chest.

"Well, that explains why you came to me first."

"Why's that?"

"You're old West, like I am," Hynes said. "Have a seat, Adams, and tell me what's on your mind."

Clint sat and said, "It's not so much what as who."

"And who would that be?"

"Clayton Black."

"Ah," Hynes said. "Not exactly Arizona's finest, is he?"

"So you know who he is?"

"Of course," Hynes said, "and I don't need to read the Chronicle to know that. He's makin' a name for himself, goin' from outlaw to fast gun in his old age." He laughed. "I should talk, though. I'm older than he is."

"Tell me," Clint said, "do you have any idea where he is?"

"Not a clue," Hynes said. "Are you changin', too? Becomin' a bounty hunter?"

"Not exactly," Clint said, "but I am looking for him." He took the clippings from his pocket. "Someone sent these to me in the mail."

Hynes accepted the clippings and took a look at them.

"Why would somebody think you're interested in Clay Black?" the lawman asked, handing them back.

"I hesitate to tell you, because it makes me sound like a fool."

"I'm listenin'."

Clint told him about tutoring Clay Black in being a better shot and faster gun.

"Did you know what he was gonna do afterward?"

"No," Clint said. "He just said he was getting older and was looking to stay alive a bit longer."

"Well," Hynes said, "I can understand that. I'd probably feel that way if I still had all my old duties as a lawman. As it is, all I do now is serve papers and jail drunks."

"I guess I'm feeling responsible for these killings," Clint said, waving the clippings.

"From what I heard, the men he killed were old partners of his, and each killin' was a fair gunfight in the street."

"Still," Clint said, pocketing the clippings, "it seems somebody is holding me responsible. I'd like to know who sent these to me."

"You check with the editor?"

"I did," Clint said. "He was no help."

"Not surprisin'," the sheriff said. "I wish I could help ya more."

"I guess I'm just happy you didn't call me a fool," Clint said.

"You musta had your reasons for helpin' him," the lawman said. "You couldn't know what he was gonna do."

"That's what I keep telling myself."

Chapter Twenty-Eight

Clint's next stop was the police department.

"We have one detective," the sergeant at the front desk told him. "He might be able to help you."

"Can I see him?"

"Sure thing," the older man said. "He's probably in the saloon across the street. His name is Detective Tillis."

"What's he look like?"

"You won't be able to miss him," the sergeant said. "He'll be drinkin' alone."

"Thanks very much."

"Sure thing."

Clint left the two-story police building and crossed to the saloon directly opposite. It was called The Whiskey Room.

As he entered, he saw that it was only about half full, as it was still early afternoon. Off to one side he saw a lone man seated at a table, leaning over a half-full beer mug and an empty shot glass. Both seemed to make him very sad. He looked around to see if there might be another likely candidate, but at the time this was the only man drinking alone. He approached the table.

"Detective Tillis?" he asked.

The man looked up at him, bleary-eyed. He had an angular face and sad eyes, looked like a tired forty-five. His grey suit had seen better days.

"Buy me a shot of whiskey and I will be," he said.

"Are you Tillis?"

"Yeah, I'm Tillis," the man said. "How about that whiskey?"

"Right away."

Clint went to the bar, came back with two beers and the shot of whiskey. He sat, pushed one beer and the shot over to Detective Tillis. The man downed the shot.

"Drink the cold one," Clint said, indicating the beer.

Tillis took two big swallows of ice-cold beer, then looked at Clint. His eyes seemed to suddenly focus.

"Who are you?" he asked.

"My name's Clint Adams."

Tillis frowned.

"I know that name," he said. "The Gunsmith, right?"

"Right."

"How'd you know who I was?"

"The sergeant across the street told me where to find you."

Tillis drank some more beer.

"What can I do for you, Mr. Gunsmith?"

"Have you heard of Clayton Black?"

"Sure."

"Do you know if he's been in town lately?"

"Whataya mean by lately?" Tillis asked.

"In the past three months?"

"Sure," Tillis said, "he was here three months ago."

"How did you know he was here?"

"I'm the police," Tillis said, "I'm supposed to know these things."

"What was he doing here?"

"I don't know."

"Who did he see while he was here?"

"I don't know."

"Did he get into any trouble while he was here?"

"I don't know."

"What *do* you know?" Clint asked.

"I know that he was here."

"How long did he stay?" Clint asked. "Do you know that?"

"A few days, no more."

A few days. That was long enough to meet and talk to David Kellogg.

"Is there anything else you can tell me?" Clint asked.

"Probably not."

"But you know about the three killings, don't you?"

"I know he gunned down three men," Tillis said, "in what were apparently fair fights. And I know none of them took place in Tucson, so they were out of our jurisdiction."

"Well, luckily," Clint said, "they weren't out of mine."

"You're going after him?"

"I've got to make this right," Clint said. "And I've got to learn a lesson."

"Stop helping people?"

"Not quite," Clint said. "I have to be careful who I give the benefit of my experience to."

Tillis lifted his beer mug and drained it.

"One more?" he asked Clint.

"Why not?"

***

After a second beer with Detective Tillis, Clint left the saloon and went back to his hotel. When he got there the desk clerk called him over.

"An envelope arrived for you, Sir," he said.

Clint accepted it. The handwriting on the front was the same, and once again there was no return address.

"Who left it here?" he asked.

"I don't know, Sir," the clerk said. "One minute there was nothing, and the next the envelope was sitting there on the desk."

"All right," Clint said. "Thank you."

It was all he could do to wait til he was in his room to open it.

Chapter Twenty-Nine

In his room he opened the envelope, wondering who had sent it and how they knew he was in Tucson. His questions weren't answered. There was just a hand-scrawled note—same handwriting as the address on the envelope—saying he "might" find what he was looking for in Bisbee, Arizona. He knew that Bisbee was just under a hundred miles from Tucson, with Tombstone right smack between them. But he had no desire to stop off in Tombstone, where the Earps and the Clantons had their O.K. Corral face-off. Things had calmed down in Tombstone since then, with Bisbee becoming more of a hot spot when the copper, gold and silver mines were discovered in the Mule Mountains. It was also a scant eleven miles north of the Mexican border.

He folded the note and set it aside, wondering if it meant he would find Clayton Black there?

More and more Clint felt like a fool for having helped Clay Black. It was apparently going to be up to him to stop the man before he killed anyone else. If that meant riding blindly into Bisbee, not knowing who had sent the note, then that's what he'd do. He was going to put a stop to the notes, the clippings, and to Clay Black.

***

He checked out of the hotel the next morning and left Tucson. He didn't bother stopping to see the sheriff, or Detective Tillis. Neither of them had been very much help to him.

He camped the first night near Benson, then bypassed Tombstone the next day, not bothering to visit the town that gave the Earps so much trouble. He was in no hurry, so he camped the next night as well, and left the last twenty miles for the daylight. He knew the Tobiano could have done it quicker, but he didn't want to push the young horse. He still had a lot of maturing to do.

He ran a brush over Toby that night, talked to the animal as he did it.

"Maybe tomorrow we'll find out who's behind all this," he said. "We'll take our time riding in, let the townspeople get a look at us. Maybe whoever sent the note will step forward. Or maybe Clay Black himself will step up." He fed the horse, tied him securely, then went to the fire and had some beans and coffee.

After he finished eating, he cleaned the plate and fork, stowed them in his saddlebag, and then poured himself another cup of coffee. Once he finished that, he turned in planning on an early departure the next morning.

***

In the morning he had only a cup of coffee, then killed the fire, packed, saddled the Tobiano and rode out.

Bisbee was smaller than Tombstone, but these days it was the busier of the two towns. The main street was pitted with the tracks of wagons traveling to and from the mines.

He reined in his horse in front of the Copper Queen Hotel and dismounted. After tying Toby to a hitching rail, he entered the hotel. The lobby was large with very high ceilings and expensive furniture.

Clint had no trouble securing a room, then left to get Toby comfortable in a livery stable. Walking back from the stable, with his saddlebags and rifle, he saw two men with badges approaching him. It seemed he wasn't going to have the option of stopping in to see the local law.

Clint decided to simply stop and wait. As the men got closer, he saw that one was in his fifties and the other in his twenties. He asked if they were sheriff and deputy.

"Hold on there, fella," the older man said.

"Sheriff," Clint said, "deputy. What can I do for you?"

"I understand you just rode into town," the older lawman said.

"That's right."

"You mind me askin' what brings you here?"

"I don't mind at all," Clint said, and stopped.

"Well?" the sheriff prodded.

"Oh, you mean you want me to tell you," Clint said. "Now?"

"Don't be a wise guy, Mister," the deputy said.

"Can it, Johnny," the sheriff said to his deputy. "Well?"

"I'm just passing through, Sheriff," Clint said. "Stopped off for a bed, a meal and a beer. Is that okay with you?"

"That depends."

"On what?"

"Who are you?"

For a moment Clint wondered if the law had been expecting him.

"My name's Clint Adams."

"Wha—" the deputy started.

"Shut up, Johnny!" the sheriff said. "Adams, if you're here lookin' for trouble—"

"Sheriff," Clint said, "I never look for trouble."

"But it pretty much finds you, don't it?" the lawman asked.

"Sometimes," Clint agreed. "Sheriff, you mind me asking your name?"

"Layne," the lawman said, "Sheriff Tyrone Layne."

"Well, Sheriff Layne," Clint said, "I was just on my way to the hotel to freshen up. Can I go?"

"How long are you plannin' on stayin' in town?" Layne asked.

"I guess that depends on how friendly folks around here are," Clint answered.

"You'll find them friendly enough," Layne said, "as long as you don't look for trouble."

Clint touched the tip of his hat and said, "Thanks for the welcome, Sheriff," and continued on.

Chapter Thirty

Clint dropped his saddlebags and rifle onto the bed then went to his window. He had a corner room. He could see the front street, but nobody would have a clear shot at him. He watched loaded wagons go one way, and empty ones come the other way. People walked the streets with purpose. Nobody was simply strolling. Bisbee was a working town.

Clint might have asked Sheriff Layne about Clay Black, but not on the street, and not in the presence of an apparently hotheaded young deputy. Maybe he would catch the man in his office at some point. He washed up, then left the room to go looking for a meal.

In a small café, while eating, he decided to visit the local post office. Rather than a counter in the mercantile, Bisbee's post office had its own building. As Clint entered, the older man behind the counter looked him over.

"Yes, can I help you?"

"I hope so," Clint said. "I have an envelope I believe was mailed from here. I'm wondering if you can tell me who mailed it?"

"I'll take a look."

Clint handed the man the envelope.

"There's no return address," the man said. "I'm afraid I can't help you, Sir." He handed it back.

"You don't recall speaking with a stranger about sending an envelope out?"

"Sorry," the man said. "I talk to so many people. But there's no post mark on this envelope. I'm guessing it was hand-delivered."

Clayton Black must have had somebody doing that.

"Okay," Clint said. "I just thought I'd take a chance."

He left the post office, decided to see if he could catch the sheriff in his office.

***

When the sheriff and his deputy got back to the office the deputy, Johnny Brown, asked, "Is that all we're gonna do?"

"What do you want to do, Johnny?" Sheriff Layne asked. "The man hasn't done anythin'."

"He's a gunman," the deputy said. "He's probably here to kill somebody."

"That ain't necessarily so," the sheriff said.

"So what are we gonna do?" Johnny asked. "Just wait?"

"I'll keep my eye on Adams," Layne said. "Meanwhile, go do your rounds."

"Yessir."

The deputy left the office, and then the sheriff poured himself a cup of coffee and sat behind his desk. He didn't like having a man like the Gunsmith in town, and hoped he wouldn't be there long. The more time he spent in Bisbee, the more chances there would be for trouble.

When his office door opened, he was surprised to see Clint Adams.

***

As Clint entered the sheriff's office, he saw the man seated at his desk, drinking coffee. He looked around and was glad not to see the deputy.

"Mr. Adams," the sheriff said. "Somethin' I can do for you?"

"I wanted to talk without your deputy around," Clint said. "He seems a little hotheaded."

"He's young," Sheriff Layne said. "Have a seat and tell me what's on your mind?"

Clint sat across from the man.

"I'm looking for Clayton Black."

"The outlaw?" Layne said. "A lot of people are lookin' for him. Do you think he's in Bisbee?"

"Somebody may want me to think he is," Clint said.

"I think you better explain that."

"Maybe I should start from the beginning."

He explained about his first meeting with Black, and then about the newspaper clippings he'd been receiving in the mail. And finally, his reason for coming to Bisbee. He showed the lawman the clippings, and the most recent note, telling him he might find what he wanted in Bisbee.

"Just as I knew you had ridden into town today," Layne said, "I think I would've noticed if Clayton Black was here. After all, he's a wanted man."

"So you don't think there's any way he could be here without you knowing it?"

"I doubt it very much," Layne said. "But . . ."

"But what, Sheriff?"

"Maybe he's on his way, and you got here first," Layne suggested.

"I guess that's possible."

"But I hope he's not comin' here," Layne said. "I don't need you and him shootin' up my streets."

"That's not my intention."

"It may not be, but you obviously feel responsible for his killin' those three men," Layne said. "And if he kills anyone else, you'll feel even worse."

"You may be right."

"So if you do happen to see him in town," Layne said, "I'd like you to tell me, and I'll handle him."

"Sheriff—"

"It's my job, Mr. Adams."

"I know, but if he guns you down—"

"That's a chance I always have to take," Layne said, cutting him off. "But I'll have Johnny with me. He may be a hothead, but he's also pretty good with a gun."

"I tell you what," Clint said, "if I do find him, I'll let you know, but you have to let me back your play."

"I guess that wouldn't hurt," Layne said, "especially if he's got other men with him. Okay, it's a deal."

"Fine. Thanks for hearing me out."

"Thanks for fillin' me in," the lawman said. "I can see where this might be weighin' on your mind. Whatever possessed you to help him in the first place?"

"My best guess is stupidity," Clint said, "pure stupidity."

"Well," Sheriff Layne said, "that affects us all at one time or another,"

"You may be right, Sheriff," Clint said, "but that doesn't make it any easier."

Chapter Thirty-One

After Clint left the sheriff's office he walked back to his hotel, thinking about what the lawman had said. It was certainly possible he had beat Clay Black to Bisbee, if the outlaw was actually headed there. There was no telling who sent those clippings and notes, or why.

Before he reached the hotel, he came to a saloon called The Queen of Hearts and decided to go in. Only a few of the tables were occupied, and there were two men standing at the bar. Clint approached and the bartender, a tall man in his mid-thirties, smiled.

"What can I get ya?" he asked.

"A beer."

"Comin' up."

The bartender drew the beer and set it down on the bar.

"Just get to town?" he asked.

"That's right," Clint said. "How could you tell?"

"You don't look like a miner."

"I'm not," Clint said. "I'm just passing through."

"You'll find Bisbee a nice place," the bartender said. "We have good, honest, hard-working people."

"I'm sure you do," Clint said.

He looked around at the other customers, who all had the look of miners.

"Is this saloon patronized by locals?" he asked.

"Pretty much," the bartender said. "That's why I was surprised you were in here."

"So where would you expect me to be?"

"Most men who are passin' through find their way to the Silver King Saloon on Waco Street."

"Then I guess that's where I'll go," Clint said, "after I finish my beer."

"It's kind of a wild place," the bartender warned. "There's usually some kinda gunplay."

"Sounds like the place I'm looking for," Clint said. "Thanks."

He paid for his beer and left.

***

Waco Street wasn't hard to find, and he saw what the bartender meant. Even the foot traffic outside the Silver King looked like everything other than miners. There were half-a-dozen horses tied up out front, three men wearing holstered pistols lounging against the front wall. Two looked to be chewing tobacco while one had a toothpick in his mouth. The three men watched as Clint approached and stepped up onto the boardwalk, but none of them said a word as he passed and went through the batwing doors.

Bisbee apparently had many visitors, as the saloon was more than half full. Most of the customers were sporting guns, either in holsters or simply tucked into their belt. This sure as hell looked like the kind of place Clay Black would drink in.

He paused inside the doors to look around, didn't spot Black at any of the tables, or at the bar. There was room at the bar for him, so he stepped up and waved at the heavyset bartender.

"Yeah?" the man said.

"Beer."

"You got money?"

Clint showed him some coins.

"I've got money."

The bartender gave him a beer, made him pay right away.

"I don't allow no tabs," he said. "Ain't no regular customers in here."

"No problem."

The beer was cold, and the glass was clean enough. He held it in his hand, turned and surveyed the room, again. There were cowboys, drifters, and hard cases. There were a couple of pretty girls working the floor.

"Lookin' for somebody?" the bartender asked, from behind him.

"Just looking," Clint said. He turned to face the man. "Why? You said there aren't any regular customers here. Do you know any of these?"

"I don't know nobody," the bartender said. "I just serve beer."

He walked off to the other end of the bar. Clint suddenly had a feeling this was his place.

Chapter Thirty-Two

While he was nursing his beer, continuing to look around, one of the girls came up to him. From what he could see, she appeared to be the older of the two, an attractive blonde with beautiful eyes and lovely, clean, smooth skin shown off by her off-the-shoulder dress.

"You look like you're lookin' for somebody, handsome," she said. "Could it be me?"

"It might be."

"I'm Peggy."

"I'm Clint."

She leaned her elbow on the bar and lounged next to him.

"Just get to town, Clint?"

"Yep, just a little while ago."

"Then you need a friend."

"You're right, I do," Clint said. "Can I buy you a drink, friend?"

"I'll take a champagne," she said, "and then we can sit at a table."

Clint went to wave at the bartender, but the man seemed to be avoiding his eye.

"I don't think the barkeep likes me," he said.

"That's Jeter," she said. "He doesn't like anybody." She turned, waved at the heavyset man, and he brought her a flute of champagne.

"A table?" she said to Clint.

"Lead the way."

She did, across the floor toward one side of the room. Clint was satisfied with the tables against the wall. Many of the men watched Peggy as she moved.

They sat across from each other.

"So, what brings you to town, Clint?"

"You were right," he said, "I'm looking for a friend of mine."

"Is he local?" she asked.

"No," Clint said, "like me, he'll be passing through."

"Then this is the place to look," she said. "Everybody in here is passing through. Even me."

"Is that right?"

"I was on my way to San Francisco, but ran out of money when I got here," she said. "So I took this job, and I've been saving my money."

"What's in San Francisco?" he asked.

"Musical theater."

"Ah, you're a singer?"

"And dancer," she said, "not that I get to do either here."

"I'll bet you're good."

"I look better than I sound," she admitted, "but I'll get my chance. I just have to get there."

"Maybe you know my friend?" he said.

"I doubt it. Like I said, everybody in here's a drifter. I don't get their names."

"You asked me for mine."

"That was different."

"Why?"

"Because you're different," she said. "I can tell."

"Different in what way?"

"You look like the kind of man I'd spend time with away from here, after work."

"Is that an invitation?" he asked.

"Could be."

He glanced around, saw the other saloon girl glowering at them from across the room.

"Why is your friend glaring at us like that?" he asked.

"Oh, we're not friends," she said. "That's Nancy. She could also tell that you're different, but I got to you before she could. That's why she's staring at us."

"She's very pretty," he said.

"If you like dark hair and dark eyes," Peggy said. "But she's too young, only about twenty-two. You need a grown woman."

"I can't argue with that," Clint said.

"But go ahead," she said, "tell me his name."

"Clayton Black."

She didn't even hesitate, which made him believe she was telling the truth when she said, "Never heard of him."

"I see."

"By the way," she said. "What's your full name?"

"It's Clint Adams."

Her eyebrows went up.

"Well," she said, "I've certainly heard of you."

"I was afraid you might."

"You're the Gunsmith," she said, "and you're looking for this Clayton Black. Do you want to kill him?"

"No, I don't."

"You have that reputation," she said, "but I don't get the feeling that you like to kill."

"I don't."

She finished her champagne and stood up.

"I'm finished here at midnight," she said, "if you're interested."

"I'll remember."

She smiled and went to entertain some other customers.

Chapter Thirty-Three

Clint finished his beer, continuing to eye the other customers as they arrived and left. There was no sign of Clayton Black, but that didn't mean he didn't have friends in the place. Black was not the kind of man who traveled alone. He usually had partners—apparently until he decided to get rid of them.

As the saloon became more and more crowded, Clint tired of sitting there, waiting. There were other saloons in town, and Clayton Black could have been in one of them. This one just seemed to be the most likely. As his stomach began to rumble, he decided to go and get himself some dinner before it got much later, and the restaurants closed.

He found a likely place several blocks from Waco Street and stopped in. When eating in a strange place, steak seemed the safest way to go. The thing about beef was, rare or well done, it was edible.

In this case it came well done. It wasn't Clint's favorite, but it filled his belly, and the coffee was strong and black.

After dinner he went back to his hotel, but after sitting in his room for almost two hours, he became bored.

Remembering that he had an invitation, he left the hotel and went back to Waco Street.

***

He got to the saloon at a quarter-to-midnight and ordered a beer from Jeter, who was busy with a crowded bar.

"Well, you're back."

He turned and saw the dark-haired girl, Nancy, looking up at him. Unlike the statuesque Peggy, this girl was small.

"I got thirsty," he said.

"Maybe you came back to see me," she suggested. "Peggy hogged your attentions, last time."

"I'm sorry, Nancy, but I'm here to see Peggy."

"But she's done for the night," Nancy said.

"I know it."

"Oh, I get it," Nancy said. "I knew she was like the others."

"What do you mean?"

"Taking money to . . . entertain men."

"You don't do that?"

"Of course not," the girl said. "I'm no whore!"

"Neither is Peggy," Clint said. "We're just going for a walk. I'm not giving her any money."

"Right," Nancy said, doubtfully.

"You should mind your own business, Nancy."

Clint looked up and saw Peggy standing there, dressed in a more modest dress than when he last saw her. He stood up.

"Are you ready to go?" he asked.

"I am," Peggy said. "Nancy, you better go back to work."

Clint and Peggy left the saloon as Nancy went back to work.

"Where to?" Clint asked.

"Unless I'm mistaken," Peggy said, "your hotel?"

"You're not mistaken."

***

As soon as they entered Clint's room, Peggy turned and rushed into his arms.

"I made up my mind I'd end up here even before I found out your full name," she said.

"And why's that?"

"Well, for one thing I was drawn to you," she said. "And for another, all those other men are pigs."

Clint kissed her soundly, the kiss going on for some time before they parted, both breathless.

They began to disrobe simultaneously, both feeling great pleasure as each of their bodies came into view. She had high, firm breasts and a lovely triangle of golden hair between her smooth thighs. She caught her breath when his hard cock appeared, jutting from between *his* thighs.

When they came together again for another kiss, their bodies burned each other. His cock was a hot column of flesh crushed between them, and she enjoyed the feel of it against her.

They fell onto the bed, still pressed together, and rolled there for a time, becoming acquainted with each other's charms. She spent time with her face between his legs, sucking him until he was good and wet. And then he took his turn, spending time on her fragrant pussy until it was soaked not only from his saliva, but from her own juices, as well.

From that point he mounted her, and she happily spread her legs for him. He drove his cock into her, and she gasped with pleasure. She wrapped her arms and legs around him, moaning as he pounded away at her. He continued to drive into her until he felt his release rush up from his thighs and explode into her . . .

***

"That was worth the wait," she said breathlessly, as they lay together, her head on his shoulder.

"It wasn't much of a wait," he said.

She laughed.

"Longer for me than you," she said. "I spotted you as soon as you walked into the saloon. And I had to move quickly, because Nancy also had her eye on you."

"Well," Clint said, "she still has time."

"You bastard," Peggy snapped, pinching him. "For as long as you're in Bisbee, you're mine. Got it?" She grabbed hold of his cock.

"Got it!" he assured her.

Chapter Thirty-Four

When Clint came down for breakfast the next morning, he found Sheriff Layne waiting in the lobby. Peggy had awakened early and left to go back to her own room at the saloon.

"Good morning, Sheriff," Clint greeted. "Waiting for me?"

"I just thought I'd check and see if you had any success findin' your man, or information that might lead you to him."

"I haven't found him," Clint said, "but I did find the Silver King on Waco Street."

Sheriff Layne scowled.

"I should've told you about that place," he said. "It's most likely the saloon you'd find him in."

"Well, he wasn't there yesterday," Clint said. "I'll have to try again today. But while you're here, how about some breakfast?"

"That sounds good, but not here," Layne said. "I'll show you a better place."

"Great," Clint said. "Lead on."

They left the hotel, and the sheriff showed the way to a small café.

***

The sheriff was greeted as if he was family. The waiter showed them to a table, ignoring all the other breakfast customers.

"This is Clint, Jerry," Layne said, as they sat. "I told him you serve the best breakfast in town."

The white-haired, sixtyish waiter smiled and said, "So now you want us to prove it to him."

"Yes," Layne said, "we'll have two of your breakfast skillets."

"Comin' up, Sheriff."

The waiter hurried away to the kitchen

"So," Clint said, "what did I do to deserve this?"

"Let's just say I don't think I was fair to you at our first meetin'," Layne said. "Or our second. I understand how reputations can get . . . overblown."

"That's okay," Clint said. "Most people—most lawmen—react to me the same way. What's your deputy think?"

"That he and I should run you out of town."

"He's anxious to try?"

"Oh yeah," Layne said. "I've practically had to sit on him to keep him from confronting you."

"You said he's good with a gun."

"And one day he might be as good as you," Layne said. "But he's not there, yet."

"Let's just hope he stays alive long enough to get there," Clint said.

"With that in mind," Sheriff Layne said, "I was wondering if . . . well, would you talk to him? Maybe getting to know you a bit better would help him learn to . . . slow down. He's in too much of a hurry to prove himself."

"He's young. But sure," Clint said. "When and where would you want me to do it?"

"I can have him in the Queen of Hearts tonight," Layne said. "He'll be a good lawman, Adams. I just have to smooth off the rough edges."

"I'll see if I can say something to him that's helpful," Clint said.

"I'd appreciate that."

The waiter brought out two skillets heaped with eggs, potatoes, ham, sausage, peppers and onions. He poured them each a cup of coffee and left the pot on the table, next to a basket of rolls.

"Anythin' else, Sheriff?" the waiter asked.

"This is perfect, Jerry."

"Enjoy, gents."

They started eating, and Clint found, with the rolls, that it was a two-handed job.

"So?" Layne asked.

"It's delicious," Clint said.

"At least you'll enjoy something while you're in Bisbee," Layne said.

Clint nodded and didn't tell the lawman about his night with Peggy.

***

After breakfast Clint walked with the sheriff as far as the man's office. Layne peered in the window.

"Johnny's inside," he said.

"You want me to come in with you?"

"No," Layne said, "I don't want to surprise him. By the time we get to the saloon tonight, he'll know you're gonna be there."

"All right, then," Clint said, "I'll see you both to-night. Thanks for breakfast."

"Any time," the lawman said, "but feel free to go there without me."

"Don't worry," Clint assured the man, "now that I know where it is, I will."

Clint watched the man go into his office, and then walked on.

Chapter Thirty-Five

Agua Prieta, Mexico

Clayton Black was eating his breakfast of enchiladas and refried beans when the sheriff of Agua Prieta walked into the cantina. The two men seated with him, also eating, stopped and looked at the man. He was a large man in his forties, with an expansive belly and pointed beard.

"Señor," the sheriff said, "I am Francisco de la Vasquez. I am *alguacil* here."

Black looked at one of his men, Paco Banderas.

"He is the sheriff," Paco translated.

"Si," de la Vasquez said, "I am sheriff."

"I'm eatin' my breakfast, Sheriff," Black said. "Whataya want?"

"Señor, you killed a man in my streets yesterday," the lawman said. "You must leave town, *por favor*."

"I can't do that right now, Sheriff," Black said. "I'm involved with somethin' and I need to be here, near the border."

"Señor, you can cross the border and go to Bisbee. You will still be near the border."

"I should've said," Black replied, "I need to be on this side of the border. Besides, I killed the man in a fair fight."

"Señor, that man, he was not a gunman," the lawman said. "He had no chance against you. It was *homicidio*."

"Murder," Paco translated.

Black stopped chewing and stared at the sheriff.

"That's a harsh word," he said.

"It was a harsh act, Señor," the lawman said. "*Por favor*, you must leave."

"Forget it," Black said, going back to his breakfast.

"Señor, I cannot, as you say, forget it," de la Vasquez said. "I must insist."

Black looked at the gun the man was wearing on his hip.

"The only way you're gonna get me to leave," he said, "is to use that gun. Can you do that?"

"If I must," the sheriff said.

"Well then, you must," Black said. "Out on the street, after my breakfast."

"Señor—"

"Be on the street, Sheriff," Black said, "and be ready."

"Si, Señor," the sheriff said. "I will be ready."

He turned and left the cantina.

"Boss," the other man, Sam Powell, said, "are you sure you wanna do that? I mean, kill a lawman."

"A Mexican lawman, Sam," Clay Black said. "That ain't no lawman, at all."

***

Clint spent the afternoon in the Silver King Saloon, waiting to see if Clay Black would walk in. During the day neither Nancy nor Peggy were working the floor. They would come down in the early evening. Before that happened, though, Clint left to keep his appointment with Sheriff Layne and the young deputy at the Queen of Hearts Saloon.

He didn't know if he was going to do any good, talking to the deputy. In fact, he didn't even know why he had agreed to help. Helping somebody was what had gotten him into this mess of a situation. But this time the request for help had come from a lawman, not an outlaw. Hopefully, that would make a difference.

***

"We're goin' where?" Johnny Brown asked his boss.

"To the Queen of Hearts," Sheriff Layne said, "to have a drink with Clint Adams."

"We're gonna drink with the Gunsmith?" the deputy asked. "And then kick him outta town?"

"He hasn't done nothin' to get kicked out of town for, Johnny," Layne said.

"He's a gunfighter," Brown said. "Ain't that reason enough?"

"No," Layne said, "it ain't."

"Then why are we gonna drink with him?" the younger man asked.

"I just thought you ought to get to know him as a man," Layne said, "and not as a reputation."

"Sheriff—"

"And don't do anythin' stupid, Johnny," Layne said, cutting him off. "We're just goin' to have a drink with the man. Understand?"

"No, Sheriff," the deputy said, "I don't understand, at all."

"Well," Layne said, "we're goin', anyway."

***

Clint was seated at a table when the two lawmen walked in. He could tell from the look on the young man's face that he wasn't happy.

They got a beer each and crossed the room to join him at the table.

Chapter Thirty-Six

"Clint Adams," Layne said, "meet Johnny Brown."

"We met," Brown said, shortly.

"On the street," Clint said, "not formally. Hello, Deputy."

"Yeah," Brown said, as he and the sheriff sat. "Look, I don't know why we're here."

"It's simple," Clint said. "Your sheriff wants to keep you from getting yourself killed."

"By you?" Brown demanded. "I'll stand out in the street with you right now!"

Clint laughed.

"What's funny?" the deputy demanded.

"This is exactly what the sheriff is afraid of," Clint said. "Your big mouth and big ego will get you killed, kid. You can't possibly stand against me."

"Are you afraid?" the deputy asked.

Clint laughed again.

"Stop laughin' at me!" Deputy Brown snapped.

"I've got to laugh," Clint said. "Look, you're young, I'll give you that. And you might be fast, but you've got no experience. You've got to take your time, kid."

"I can do anythin' you can do," the kid said.

Clint called over a saloon girl.

"Yes, Sir?"

"Can you bring me a couple of poker chips, please?"

"Yessir."

"We gonna play poker?" the kid asked.

"No, but we are going to play a game," Clint said.

The girl came over with a blue chip, and a red one.

"Thank you," Clint said. He pushed the chips over to Sheriff Layne. "Toss one into the air."

"In here?"

"Don't worry," Clint assured him, "nobody will get hurt."

"Well, all right."

Layne picked up a blue chip and tossed it into the air. Clint drew and fired from his seated position. The poker chip hit the floor and everyone fell silent and looked. Layne walked over and picked up the chip, brought it back to the table. He showed it to Clint and Johnny Brown.

"A hole right through the middle," he said.

"Now the red chip is yours, kid," Clint said.

Brown licked his lips and said to the sheriff, "Toss it."

Layne picked up the red chip and tossed it up. Brown drew and fired. The chip hit the floor. Layne went and got it, brought it back. As he showed it to Clint and Johnny Brown, there was a nick off to the side.

"Off center," Layne said.

"But I hit it!" Brown pointed out.

"The point was to hit it in the center," Clint said. "I'm impressed that you did hit it, but you need more experience."

"Could you do it again?" Brown asked.

"Every time," Clint said.

"I—I think I could do it."

"Every time?" Clint asked.

"Well . . . no."

"You've got to be able to do it every time, Johnny," Clint said.

The conversations around them started up again.

"You need to practice," Clint said, "and not be impatient to face another gun. The sheriff tells me you're going to be a good lawman, some day. And I think you're going to be a top gun, but it's years away."

"You really think so?"

"Not too many people would have been able to hit that poker chip," Clint said. "You're going to get there, Johnny."

Johnny Brown's demeanor softened, and for the next hour he, Clint and the sheriff just talked. The kid asked a lot of questions, which to Clint was a good sign.

Finally, Sheriff Layne said, "Johnny, you better go and make your rounds."

"Yessir." He stood up. "Uh, thanks, Mr. Adams."

"Sure, kid."

Brown left the saloon.

"I gotta thank you for that," Sheriff Layne said. "I think you straightened him out."

"I hope so," Clint said.

"And now that's done," Layne said, "I've got some news for you that you might or might not like."

"About what?"

"Your man, Clay Black."

"You heard something about him?"

Layne nodded.

"He killed two men south of the border, in a town called Agua Prieta."

"Who?"

"A caballero," Layne said, "and the local sheriff."

"He killed a lawman?"

Layne nodded.

"Right in the street," the lawman said.

"Is he still there?"

"From what I heard, yes," Layne said.

"He's the one who wanted me in Bisbee, then," Clint said. "So I could hear this."

"But why?" Layne asked. "He knows you'll come after him."

"He wants me to come after him," Clint said. "He's worse than Johnny, Sheriff. He wants to prove himself against me."

"Are you goin'?"

"First thing in the morning," Clint said. "It's time to end this."

Chapter Thirty-Seven

Clint checked out of his hotel the next morning after bidding Peggy a farewell in bed the night before. He saddled Toby and headed south for the Mexican border.

Agua Prieta was not far, not even a day's ride. There was no reason for him to camp overnight. His only hope was that Black would still be there when he arrived.

He was now convinced that the clippings and notes had all been sent to him by Clayton Black. Once Black convinced himself that he was faster, better than he used to be—by having killed the three partners who were after him—he must have decided to test himself against Clint. Now he had killed a lawman, dead sure that would bring Clint to him.

From the short time he had known Black, though, he was sure the man would not be alone. He had no idea if he was riding into a situation where he'd face three men, or a dozen, or something in-between, but he felt sure Clay Black's ego would make him face Clint man-to-man in the street. After that, who knew what would happen?

He'd find out soon enough.

***

He rode into Agua Prieta, a small, sleepy Mexican town, before dark. Nobody seemed to be paying any attention to him.

He spotted the sheriff's office and decided to stop there and see if there was a deputy. He dismounted and entered the office. There was a man seated at the desk, his hat pulled down over his eyes, feet up, snoring lightly.

Clint slammed the door.

The man came awake, banging his feet down onto the floor. His sad face had a puzzled look on it. Clint figured him for a worn out thirty-five.

"Are you the sheriff?" Clint asked.

"The sheriff is dead, Señor," the man said.

"Then you're the deputy?"

"Si, Señor. Can I help you?"

"I'm looking for the man who killed your sheriff."

"Ah, the gringo outlaw," the deputy said. "He has a room behind the cantina."

"Why isn't he in your jail?"

"Señor, I am the deputy," the man said, "but I am not a fool. I do not want to die."

"So he's just walking free?"

The man shrugged.

"It was a fair fight, Señor."

"Sure it was. Who's he got with him?"

"Ah, two other men. They are always by his side."

"Are you sure he's still in town?"

"I am not."

"Then I'll have to find out."

"Do you intend to kill this man?"

"I intend to see to it that he doesn't kill anyone else," Clint said.

"And you can do that without killing him?"

"That remains to be seen," Clint said. "I'm going to go to the cantina to see him. Where will you be?"

"I will be here, Señor," the man said, with a shrug.

"Hiding?"

"Si, Señor," the deputy said, "hiding and staying alive."

"You just keep doing that, deputy," Clint said, and left.

***

Clint rode directly to the cantina. There was no point in putting the Tobiano in a livery stable if he could finish this within minutes. All he had to do was find that Clayton Black was still there.

He tied the horse off outside and entered the little cantina. The few Mexicans seated at tables looked at him curiously, then looked away. They had probably seen enough trouble with gringos.

"Señor?" a pretty, black-haired girl said, "you wish a table? Or a room?"

"I wish to see one of your guests." Clint said.

"Who, Señor?"

"Clayton Black," Clint said, "the man who killed your sheriff."

"Oh, Señor . . ."

"What is it?"

"Señor Black is not here," she said. "You are perhaps Señor Adams?"

"I am."

"He left a note for you Señor." She took it from her apron and handed it to him

"Thanks."

"Do you wish something to drink?"

"Yes," Clint said, "cerveza."

She smiled.

"One beer coming up, Señor."

He sat at a table and unfolded the note.

Chapter Thirty-Eight

He recognized the handwriting right away. It confirmed what he had already decided, that Clayton Black had sent the clippings and previous notes. This one said: YOU ALMOST MADE IT. SEE YOU SOON.

The girl brought him his beer.

"Would you like some food?" she asked.

"Yes," he said, "and apparently, I'll need a room."

"As you wish, Señor," she said, "but first the food. What shall I bring you?"

"Surprise me."

She smiled.

"Very good, Señor."

She went to the kitchen and came back with platters of rice and meat and rolled up tortillas.

"Thank you," he said.

"*Por nada*, Señor."

"Can you sit a minute?" he asked.

"Si, Señor, if you wish."

"What's your name?"

"Carmen, Señor."

"Carmen, the gringo Clayton Black, did you spend any time with him?"

"No, Señor," she said, "I only serve him food and drink."

"And his friends?"

"Si, Señor."

"Do you remember their names?"

"I heard him call one Paco."

"And when he left here," Clint asked, rolling the meat into a tortilla, "did they leave with him?"

"Si, Señor."

"Do you know any girls who spent time with Clayton Black in his room?"

"Si, Señor," she said. "There was Fatima."

"Ah," Clint said, "and where would I find Fatima?"

"I can send her to your room, Señor." He thought she looked disappointed. Carmen was very pretty, appeared to be in her twenties.

"Carmen," he said, "I only want to talk to her. Please make sure she knows that."

Carmen brightened.

"Oh, si, Señor. But . . ."

"But what?"

"I am afraid you will still have to pay her."

"I'll be happy to pay her," he said.

"I will have her come to your room," she said. "When you have finished eating, I will take you there."

"Thank you, Carmen."

***

The food was good enough for him to ask for seconds, and then Carmen took him down a hallway to a room.

"Which room was Clayton Back's?" he asked.

"That one," she said, pointing to the door across from him.

"Can I get a look inside?" he asked.

"It is not locked," she told him "I will send Fatima to you tonight."

"Good," he said. "I have to take care of my horse."

"There is a livery stable at the end of the street," she said. "My cousin, Jesus, runs it. Mention my name."

"I will. Thank you."

He left the hotel to take care of the Tobiano first. Carmen's cousin assured him that he would take good care of the animal.

Clint took his saddlebags and rifle to his room, then crossed the hall to the room Clayton Black had occupied. He doubted the man had left anything behind, but he spent the time looking, anyway.

A quick search of the room revealed nothing. His only chance after that was if this Fatima could tell him something useful. He went back to his room to wait.

***

He had a copy of some Edgar Allan Poe's stories with him and sat on the bed reading while he waited. He set it aside when there was a knock at his door. He was still wearing his gun when he walked to it.

"Who is it?" he asked

"Fatima, Señor."

He opened the door, saw a dark-haired, full-bodied woman in her thirties standing there. She wore a plain skirt and peasant blouse.

"Carmen told me you wanted to talk to me, Señor," she said. "And that you would pay."

"That's right," he said. "Won't you come in."

She stepped inside. He looked up and down the hall before closing the door.

"I'm sorry," he said. "I have nothing to offer you to drink."

"That is all right, Señor," she assured him. "As long as you pay."

"Of course." He took out some money and handed it to her. She smiled and accepted it.

"Now let us talk," she said.

Chapter Thirty-Nine

"Carmen tells me you spent time with Clayton Black," Clint said.

"Si Señor," she said. "He was a brutal man."

"I'm sorry he hurt you," Clint said. "I can make him pay for it when I find him."

"You will kill him?"

"Probably."

"Good!" She spat dryly.

"But before I can do that," he said, "I need to find him. Did he give you any idea where he'd be going from here?"

"No," she said.

"Are you sure?"

"He did not talk," she said, "except to tell me what he wanted me to do, or what he was going to do."

"What about his two men?" he asked. "Did you hear them talk?"

"No."

"Damn!"

"But maybe the other girls . . ."

"There were other girls?"

"Yes," Fatima said. "Sofia and Salma. They stayed with the other men."

"Can you bring them to me?" he asked.

"To talk?"

"Yes," he said, "to talk. And I'll pay them."

"I will bring them. Tonight?"

"Please," he said. "I'll stay right here."

"Will you pay me again?"

"Yes."

She headed for the door.

"I will be back."

She slipped out of the room. He went back to Poe.

***

The next time a knock came at the door he sensed more than one person.

"Who is it?" he asked.

"Fatima," she said. "I have Sofia and Salma with me."

He opened the door, saw the three women standing there. Sofia and Salma were tall, dark and lean, and looked enough alike to be sisters.

"Come in," he invited.

As they entered one of them said, "Fatima, you did not tell us this one would be so handsome."

"You are here to talk," Fatima said, "nothing more."

Both of them pouted.

"You're sisters," Clint said.

"We are," one said.

"Twins," the other said.

"Ah."

"I am Sofia," one said.

"And I am Salma."

"What do you want to talk about?" Sofia asked. "Or was it Salma.

"The two men you stayed with," he said. "What were their names?"

"Paco," Salma said. "Mine was Paco."

"Sam," Sofia said, "mine's name was Sam Powell. He was . . . tender."

"Not Paco," Salma said. "He was mean."

"Did either of these men give you any idea where they'd be going from here?" Clint asked.

"Not Paco," Salma said. "He did not talk."

"What about this Sam Powell?" Clint asked Sofia. "Did he say anything?"

"He said one thing."

"What was it?"

The sisters looked at each other.

"Fatima said you would pay."

Clint took out some money and gave them each some. Happily, they tucked the bills away.

"What did Sam Powell say?" Clint asked.

"He said the other man, Clayton Black, was going to kill the Gunsmith, and make them all famous and rich," Sofia said. "You are the Gunsmith?"

"I am."

"He said it would all come to an end in Nogales."

Nogales was to the west, still just over the border in Mexico.

"He said that?"

She nodded.

"All right," Clint said. "Thank you, ladies."

"That is all you want, Señor?" Fatima asked. "You are sure?"

"I'm positive."

He ushered all three of them out and closed the door.

The information about Nogales was a message from Clay Black. Of that, he was sure. The man was still leading him around by the nose, but that was all right. Because when he finally found him, he'd show Black the error of his ways.

And he was sure that was going to happen in Nogales.

Chapter Forty

Nogales was less than a day's ride, so Clint rode down the main street in the early evening. It was a lively border town, with Americans coming and Mexicans going. Its income was derived from gambling, drinking and women. For these reasons, saloons lined each side of the street. Music and laughter drifted out over the batwing doors, as drunken bodies came hurling through them into the street. Clint had to stop abruptly, to keep from trampling one or two. He looked down, hoping against hope that one of the men would turn out to be Clayton Black, but that wasn't the case.

This time Clint decided to board the Tobiano and get a hotel room first, then decide what to do.

Once he had his saddlebags and rifle in his room, he thought the proper move would be to see the sheriff—as long as he could get to the man before Clayton Black killed him.

He found the sheriff's office, a box-like, adobe structure with a very heavy wooden door. As he entered, a man holding a coffee cup and wearing a badge turned to look at him. At least he was alive, and not sleeping at his desk. He was a tall, handsome Mexican in his forties with a carefully trimmed, pencil thin mustache.

"Señor," he said, "may I help you?"

"My name's Clint Adams, Sheriff," Clint said, "and I'm in Nogales looking for someone."

"I am Sheriff Carlos de la Plata. You are Clint Adams, the Gunsmith?"

"That's right."

"And this man you are looking for," the sheriff went on, "you intend to kill him?"

"That's going to be up to him."

"And what has this man done?"

"Well," Clint said, "among other things, he just recently killed the sheriff of Agua Prieta."

"Sheriff Vasquez is dead?"

"I'm afraid so."

The lawman frowned.

"That is disturbing. He was a good man. Who is this man who killed him?"

"His name's Clayton Black."

"Ah, a gringo."

"Yes."

"And an outlaw?"

"Very definitely, yes."

The sheriff sipped his coffee.

"Well," he said, after a moment, "as long as you don't kill anyone else, I do not have a problem with this."

"Okay, but there might be a slight problem."

"What is it?"

"He will probably have two men with him."

"And you will be forced to kill them?"

"Possibly."

The sheriff sipped his coffee again.

"Señor, as long as you are not expecting me to stand with you," the lawman said, finally, "I do not have a problem with that either."

"I have one other question," Clint said.

"What's that?"

"I'm staying at the Hacienda Hotel," Clint said. "Should I eat there or somewhere else?"

"I suggest you eat at the Rosa Blanca Cantina, two blocks east of your hotel."

"Much obliged."

"Señor," the sheriff said as Clint turned toward the door.

"Yes?"

"Is there a possibility that these three men will kill you, instead of you killing them?"

"There's always a possibility, Sheriff."

"I would not like that."

"I appreciate that."

"If they kill you," he went on, "I would be forced to take some action."

"Do you have deputies?"

"I have one," the sheriff said, "but his specialty is siesta time." He heaved a great sigh. "I suppose I will have to hire at least two more."

"It may take me a day or two to find my man," Clint said.

"Gracias," Sheriff de la Plata said, "I will be ready by then."

Clint left the office.

***

The Rosa Blanca Cantina was easy to find, as people were going in and out as Clint arrived. It was apparently a popular border eatery. When Clint got inside, he saw that the place extended well back with plenty of room for the crowd. A table in the rear was a simple request for them to grant.

"What would the señor like to eat?" the waiter asked.

"Tacos," Clint said.

"Si, Señor," the waiter said.

The tacos came with refried beans and rice, and Clint proceeded to wash it all down with two glasses of beer.

Chapter Forty-One

There was a question Clint should have asked the sheriff, so he decided to try it on the waiter.

"What's the most popular saloon in town for gringos?"

"Oh, Señor," the waiter said, "this is Nogales. All the saloons serve Mexicans and gringos." The man shrugged his shoulders. "Take your pick."

"Gracias," Clint said. He paid for his meal and left.

It was getting dark, which meant the saloons were starting to light up. There were probably more saloons per square foot in Nogales than Clint had seen in any other town. All he could do was start walking and peer into them one-by-one.

They all had bat wing doors, which made it easy for the drunks to be tossed out. He looked in over the doors, counting on his senses to pick and choose the saloons he should stop into. From the doors he was able to see which places had the most gringos, and those were the ones he went into and ordered a beer at the bar.

Most of the saloons were cheap, with cheap looking girls working the floor. In a couple of them the glasses were actually too dirty for Clint to drink out of, so he just left the beers on the bar.

He had a feeling Clayton Black wouldn't patronize the very cheap places, so he started looking for saloons that offered better quality girls and drinks.

He didn't bother checking the gaming tables, because the entire time he had spent with Black, the man never even mentioned gambling.

He finally found a place where the beer looked safe to drink, and the girls looked clean enough to—well, they were clean.

He doubted he would be able to find Black his first night in town. Of course, there was always the chance the man would find him. That might have been the strategy he should employ the next day. Make it clear who he was, where he was staying, where he was drinking, and wait. After all, Clayton Black wanted to try his skills against the Gunsmith. That was what this was all about.

The saloon he finally settled on was called The Red Boot. It had a red boot over the door, and the painting of a naked girl wearing one red boot over the bar.

While he nursed his beer and looked around, one of the girls came over. She was American, with red hair, green eyes and a wide smile. All of that was offset by a green dress.

"Are you lookin' for somebody?"

"I'm just looking to see if a friend of mine is here," Clint said.

"Is your friend American, or Mexican?"

"American," Clint said, "but he might have a Mexican with him."

"I ain't gonna ask you his name," she said, "because it wouldn't matter."

"I didn't think it would."

"You want some company while you wait?"

"Thanks, but I don't think so."

"Suit yerself," she said. "Good luck."

The girl went off to find other prey.

Clint turned to the bartender and waved for another beer.

"Why is this the only place in town with clean glasses?" he asked the man.

The bartender, a pleasant-faced man in his forties, smiled and said, "Somebody's gotta have 'em."

"Well, I'm glad I found you," Clint said.

"Tell you what," the barkeep said, "I'll make this second one on the house."

"Much obliged," Clint said.

He nursed his complimentary beer, had a third that he paid for, then packed it in and went to his hotel.

Chapter Forty-Two

In the morning Clint returned to the Rosa Blanca Cantina for breakfast. The waiter brought him a plate of *huevos rancheros* and a pot of coffee. He ate the meal slowly, enjoying every bite. If it hadn't been for Clayton Black, he would probably have enjoyed some time in Nogales. The place was lively, and he hadn't really gambled seriously in some time. Lately, he found himself thinking about sitting at a poker table.

Of course, after possibly killing Clayton Black and his two partners, there would be no way he could stay in town. The sheriff certainly wouldn't want him around.

He figured he better take his time and enjoy this meal while he could.

***

Paco knocked on the door, and when Clayton Black opened it, he said, "He is here, jefe."

"Where?"

"He has a room at the Hacienda," Paco said.

"Are you sure?"

"Señor Sam and I were watching for him," Paco said. "He is at the Hacienda, and he is eating at the Rosa Blanca Cantina. Señor Sam is watching him, now."

"Did you tell him to stay out of sight?"

"Si, Señor."

Paco looked past Black at the naked girl on the bed. She was American and appeared to have red welts on her pale skin.

"All right," Black said to the Mexican, "wait downstairs for me."

"Si, Señor."

As Black closed the door, Paco heard him say, "Now where were we?"

***

Clayton Black and Paco joined Sam Powell across the street from the Rosa Blanca Cantina.

"Where is he?" Black asked.

"Still inside, eating," Powell said. "We can get 'im when he comes out. He'll never know what hit 'im."

"We're not doin' that," Black said. "That's not the reason we got 'im here."

"But boss—"

"Just shut up and wait here."

"Where ya goin'?"

"To talk to an old friend," Black said, and walked across the street.

***

Clint was not surprised to see Clayton Black enter the cantina. Even from his back table he had been able to see out the door, and across the street, where a man was watching. If that man had followed him from his hotel, then he had been careless and was lucky to be alive.

Clayton Black smiled as he approached Clint's table. Clint looked at the gun and holster he had supplied Clayton Black with.

"Well, if it isn't my old friend, Mr. Adams," the outlaw said. "Mind if I sit?"

"Not at all, Black," Clint said. "Have some coffee."

"I think I will," Black said, pouring it for himself. "I've seen this place. How's the food?" He looked down at Clint's empty plate.

"Very good."

"I'll have to try it."

"You've led me a merry chase, Black," Clint said. "With the clippings and the notes."

Black laughed.

"Just a game, Adams, just a game," he said.

"And is the game over, now?"

"I'm afraid so."

"Let me pay my bill," Clint said. "I'll meet you outside."

"No, no," Black said, "not yet. I have two partners outside, and I can't count on them to stay out of the fight."

"Then when?"

"Later today," Black said.

"What was the idea of killing a lawman, Black?" Clint asked. "You left me no choice but to come."

"Well then," Clayton Black said, "that was the point."

"But why?"

"Thanks to you, I'm gonna live a lot longer than I might have," Black said.

"By killing?"

"Yes."

"And after you've killed me, who are you going to kill?" Clint asked.

Black grinned.

"Anybody I want."

"Then you leave me no choice," Clint said.

"Good." Black stood without touching his coffee. "Later today, then. I want to make sure it's just the two of us."

Black touched his gun, turned and walked out.

Chapter Forty-Three

Clint stopped at the sheriff's office.

"Did you find him?" the lawman asked.

"He found me," Clint said.

"Is he dead?"

"No," Clint said. "I'm supposed to meet him later."

"Where?"

"On the streets."

"What about his friends?" the lawman asked.

"He says he's going to keep them out of it," Clint said.

"Do you believe him?"

"I'm not sure," Clint said. "He wants to prove himself against me, but I can't believe he won't hedge his bet."

"Then I still need those deputies," the sheriff said.

"Wouldn't hurt to have them handy."

Clint turned to leave.

"Tell me something," the sheriff said.

"What?"

"Is there a chance he can beat you, man-to-man?"

"There's always a chance," Clint said, and walked out the door.

***

"You can't be serious," Sam Powell said to Clayton Black.

"And why not?"

They were seated at a table in a small saloon, along with Paco.

"You've seen my move," Black said.

"Well, yeah, I've seen that trick holster, but this is the Gunsmith we're talkin' about," Powell said. "Why would you go up against him alone?"

"To prove a point."

"What point?"

"That I'm the fastest," Black said.

"And that's important?"

"It is to me," Black said. "Right now, I'm just an outlaw. After I outdraw the Gunsmith, in the center of the street, I'll be a legend."

"You think that trick holster is gonna be enough?" Powell asked.

"The holster, the gun," Black said, "and my move."

Powell looked across the table at Paco, who only shrugged and drank his beer.

"When will you do this?" Powell asked.

"Later today," Black said. "I just want him to wait and think."

"And what are we supposed to do?"

"Also wait."

"No," Powell said, "I mean, while you face him. And after."

"While I face him, you watch," Black said. "After . . . well, that'll be up to you."

Powell looked at Paco.

"What do you have to say about all of this?"

"I do what I am told," Paco said.

Powell looked at Black, who smiled at him.

***

Clint wondered where Clayton Black was at that moment. If he knew, he could press the issue, make the man deal with it before he was ready.

He knew Black was making him wait, thinking it was an effective strategy. But Clint also knew that there was always a possibility that a gunfight would be his last. It was as he had told the sheriff, there was always a chance Black and his trick holster would beat him. Because he accepted that truth, he never got nervous. He knew that he would eventually die by the gun, as he had lived.

So he had to wait for Clayton Black to make his move. Letting the man take the lead would give him some false confidence. To Clint's way of thinking, the wait would play more on Black's mind than on his.

He decided to do his waiting at The Red Boot.

***

As he entered the saloon, he saw that it was far busier than it had been the last time he was there. There were actually four girls working the floor now, but he was able to spot the redhead in the green dress very easily.

He ordered a beer and as the bartender gave it to him he asked, "What's the red head's name?"

"That's Shannon," the man said. "Want me to call 'er over here?"

"I don't think you'll have to," Clint said. "She'll come on her own."

"You sound pretty sure of yourself," the man said, with a shrug.

As the bartender left him he turned, beer in hand, and looked over at Shannon. It was obvious she had seen him enter the saloon. He smiled and raised his glass to her in a salute.

She started over to him.

Behind him he heard the bartender say, "Damn."

Chapter Forty-Four

Shannon took him to an empty table in the rear of the saloon.

"I had a feeling you'd be coming back," she said.

"You did? Why's that?"

"Because I'm your type."

"And what makes you say that?"

"Easy," she said. "You're my type. We attract each other."

"You don't talk like any other saloon girl I've met," he said.

"I used to be a school teacher," she said.

"Really? What did you teach?"

"A little of everything," she said. "But I eventually got tired of dealing with children. I'd much rather deal with adults. And by that I mean, men."

"I'm not all that good with children myself," he told her.

"I'm sure you're much better with adults," she said, "and by that I mean, women."

"I like women a lot," he said.

"Would you like to show me how much?"

"I'd love to, but . . ."

"I mean, after I get off work."

"The idea appeals to me very much, but the fact is, I might not be around tonight after you get off."

"Is something going to happen between now and then?"

"Definitely."

"Well then," she said, "I guess I'll quit early today."

"Can you do that?"

She smiled.

"I'm their best girl," she said. "I can do whatever I want. Why don't you wait for me outside?"

"Now?"

"Right now," she said. "I won't be ten minutes."

"Well, okay."

They both stood. She went upstairs, and he stepped outside to wait.

***

He was outside for five minutes when three men came out, looked around, and walked over to him.

"You waitin' for Shannon?" one asked.

"That's right."

"We don't think that's a good idea," the man said. The two men with him just nodded.

"Oh? And why's that?"

"Because she's my girl."

All three wore holstered firearms and were in their thirties.

"Funny," he said, "she didn't mention having a boy-friend."

"Well, I guess maybe it skipped her mind," the man said. "But I'm tellin' ya, she's mine."

"She's going to meet me out here," Clint said. "It would be rude of me not to wait."

"I'll explain it to her," the man said. "Don't worry."

"Oh, but I do worry," Clint said. "I'd hate for the lady to think I'm rude. So I'm just going to wait for her and explain that you've warned me off."

The three men exchanged a worried glance.

"That ain't a good idea," the spokesman said.

"So maybe you're not her boyfriend?"

"I never said I was," the man replied. "I said she was mine."

"Maybe she has a different idea."

"Now Mister—"

"Jake Fielder, what the hell are you doing?" Shannon snapped as she came through the batwing doors. She was wearing the same dress but had put a shawl over her bare shoulders.

"Well, I—"

"Jake was telling me how you belong to him," Clint said.

"That's a load of hogwash!" she snapped. "I don't belong to anybody, least of all Jake." She looked at the man. "You and your friends go back inside and mind your business!"

"Aw, Shannon—"

"Go ahead! Shoo!"

At that moment, Clint saw the school teacher in her, dealing with naughty boys.

She started to take Clint's right arm, but he moved her to his left side, and they started walking away from the saloon.

"I need to keep my right arm free," he said.

"Those boys won't bother you again," she assured him.

"It's not those boys I'm thinking about," Clint said.

He could see the two men across the street, who Clayton Black probably sent to keep an eye on him. After all, the outlaw needed to know where Clint was in order to make his move.

***

"Whataya think?" Sam Powell asked Paco. "We could take 'im right now."

"That would not make Señor Black happy," Paco said. "And it might make one of us dead. I do not wish it to be me."

So they just started to follow.

Chapter Forty-Five

When they got to Clint's hotel, he stopped them in the lobby.

"What's wrong?" Shannon asked.

"I think this might be a bad idea."

"Why's that?"

"You could be in danger," Clint said. "There are two men following us, and one other waiting to kill me."

"Is that why you said we couldn't do this tonight?" she asked.

"I said might not be able to do it tonight, but yes," he answered. "I know I made you leave work early, but—"

"Don't worry about it," she said. "I'll slip out the back and go back to work. Just promise me I'll see you tonight, after work."

"If things go the way I hope they will," he said, "definitely."

She kissed his cheek and said, "Be careful."

As she headed for the hotel's back door, Clint wondered if he should go to his room to wait for Clayton Black, or just sit in the lobby?

***

"Okay," Powell said, as Clint and Shannon entered the hotel, "I'll go and tell Black they're here. You watch in case they leave."

"Si, Señor, I will watch," Paco said.

***

Powell found Black sitting in a rundown saloon called The Rusty Hinge.

"Where is he?" Black asked.

"In his hotel," Powell said, "with a saloon girl."

Black laughed.

"That's perfect." He stood up. "Come on!"

The two men left the saloon and headed for the hotel. When they reached it, Paco was still watching from across the street.

"Is he still inside?" Black asked.

"Si, Señor."

"And the woman?"

"I did not see her leave."

"Good," Black said. "This is the time for me to push him into a fight, when his pants are down."

"You want us to go in with you?" Powell asked.

"No," Black said, "just wait out here and watch."

Clayton Black stepped into the street and headed for the hotel.

***

Clint was seated in the lobby, waiting, when Black entered. He thought the man looked surprised to see him there but tried to hide it as he approached.

"I thought you'd be in your room with a girl," he said.

"I didn't think that would be such a good idea, for her," Clint said.

Black laughed.

"Did you think I'd kick in your door and come in with gun blazin'?"

"No," Clint said, "I just thought you'd try to catch me with my pants down."

He could see from the look on the outlaw's face that he had read his mind.

"Well, it don't matter," Black said. "You're here, I'm here, and there's a big, wide street out front."

"A crowded street," Clint pointed out.

"I don't mind havin' a passle of people watch."

"Tell me something, Black," Clint said. "Was this your plan all along? To use me, and then use what you got from me to kill me?"

"No," Black said, "not *all* along. But somewhere along the way it occurred to me. Why, did you think we were makin' friends?"

"Friends?" Clint asked. "No, I never thought we were friends."

"Good," Black said, "because I wouldn't want to disappoint you and have you think that a friend turned on you."

"I never felt we were going to be friends Black," Clint said, "but I do feel like I got you to make a fool out of me. Because of you I'm going to think twice from now on before I help anybody."

"If you survive, you mean," Black said.

"Oh, I'll survive," Clint said. "I may have taught you a few things, but I didn't teach you everything I know."

"I know enough," Black said.

"Usually, I give men a chance to walk away, at this point."

"The only place I'm walkin' is out that door to wait for you in the street," Black said. "Just don't make me wait too long."

"Don't worry," Clint said. "I'll be along directly."

He watched Clayton Black turn and walk back across the lobby and out the front door. He knew his two partners would also be outside, waiting.

Chapter Forty-Six

When Clint stepped out the front door, he saw Clayton Black waiting in the street. Most people knew what it meant when a man was standing in the street wearing a gun, so the area was empty, with people gathered on each side to watch. Clint also noticed that Black's two men were on either side of the street.

As Clint got closer, the onlookers thought better of their positions and started to seek cover indoors from where they could watch in safety.

The street ran north to south, so there was no position Clint could take where the sun would be at his back. Their positions in that respect would be equal.

Clint walked to the center, then turned to face Clayton Black.

"We don't have to do this, Black," he said. "All you have to do is take that gun off and give it up."

"I ain't gonna do that, Adams," Black said. "I still got a lot of life in me, and there's lots more trains and stagecoaches and banks out there."

"And men to kill?"

"Some."

Clint shook his head.

"Let's see how that trick holster works," he said.

"My pleasure."

It worked pretty well. Black went for his gun, the holster sprang open, the gun fairly jumped into his hand, but as he was bringing it up, Clint drew and shot him in the chest.

At that same moment, on both sides of the street, Paco and Sam Powell drew their guns and started firing. Clint, expecting something like this, was already moving. He dropped to one knee, whirled around and shot Paco. The bullet struck the Mexican in the belly.

As a couple of chunks of hot lead hit the street around him, he turned again and fired at Sam Powell. This time his bullet hit the man in the forehead. He was dead before he hit the ground.

It got quiet after that, except for doors opening as people stepped back out to take a closer look at what had happened. They crowded into the street to look at the bodies, and from the center of the crowd Sheriff de la Plata appeared.

"That was something to see, Señor," he said.

"Glad you enjoyed it," Clint said, reloading his gun and holstering it.

"Señor," the lawman said, "it is my job to watch."

"Not exactly what I think a lawman's job is," Clint said.

"What will you do now?" the sheriff asked.

"Get the hell out of Dodge," Clint said.

"Señor?"

"I'll be leaving Nogales first thing in the morning," Clint explained. He had kept his promise to himself to stop Clayton Black. Now he just had to keep his promise to a pretty redhead.

Coming Soon!

THE GUNSMITH
475
SIX DEADLY GUNS

For more information
visit: www.SpeakingVolumes.us

On Sale Now!

Award-Winning Author
Robert J. Randisi (J.R. Roberts)

**For more information
visit:**